THE LION WITHIN

CATAMOUNT LION SHIFTERS, BOOK 6

J.H. CROIX

DEDICATION

To all the readers out there who enjoy taking a step beyond our world! Who's to say what creatures walk among us?

Sign up for my newsletter for information on new releases!
http://jhcroixauthor.com/subscribe/

Follow me!
jhcroix@jhcroix.com
https://amazon.com/author/jhcroix
https://www.bookbub.com/authors/j-h-croix
https://www.facebook.com/jhcroix
https://www.instagram.com/jhcroix/

ONCE UPON A TIME...

Centuries ago in the northern Appalachian Mountains, mountain lions fled deeper and deeper into the mountains, seeking safety from the rapid encroachment of humanity into their vast territory. Mountain lions developed the power to shift from human to mountain lion and back again, saving their species as they hid in plain sight. The majestic wild cats became creatures of myth in the East while they flourished out West. Everywhere they were known as ghost cats because they were rarely encountered in the wild and moved with prowess and stealth. The wild cats expanded their range as their shifter ancestors intermingled with them, deepening the circle of protection for the species with layer upon layer of secrecy. The infamous ghost cats had powers of stealth beyond what most people imagined. Yet, their safety relied on a contract that couldn't be broken among shifters—they must protect the secret of their existence. In recent years, this contract had weakened due to the greed and misplaced pride of a few shifters. The unprecedented success of shifters at hiding in plain sight over centuries had emboldened some who thought secrecy was no longer necessary.

1

"Watch out!"

Sophia Ashworth glanced up at the sound of her friend's voice to see a potted tulip tottering on the deck railing just above her head. She had been looking down at the slate walkway that wound around the deck at her friend Vivian's house. Her eyes followed the bright red tulip as it lurched from side to side before it toppled off the railing. With a squeal, she dashed out of the way. She managed to avoid getting conked on the head, but her shoulder was covered in potting soil when she looked up again. The plant pot sat cracked on the ground. She glanced up at Vivian to find her covering her mouth in a weak attempt to keep from laughing aloud.

Sophia rolled her eyes and brushed the soil off her shoulder before sifting her fingers through her hair. The tulip hung from the back of her hair. Carefully untangling it, she noticed its bulb had survived the fall. She held it aloft as she walked up the stairs to the deck.

"After all that, you'd better replant this poor flower."

She handed the bedraggled tulip to Vivi and glanced around. "How the hell did that happen?"

Vivi had given up from holding back her laugh and simply pointed over at her cat, a black and white cat who was just barely past being a kitten.

Sophia strode over to the cat and swept him in her arms. "Jax, you are trouble!" She nuzzled her nose in his neck. His return purr was enough to vibrate through her entire body. Holding Jax in her arms, Sophia plopped down in a chair beside the small wooden table on her friend's deck.

Vivian Sheldon, Vivi to her friends and family, was Sophia's best friend. Lately, Sophia needed lots of Vivi time. Her brother Heath had been arrested two months ago when he was caught at a local drug dealer's house in the middle of buying heroin. At thirty-one, Heath was three years older than Sophia and had been her beloved older brother her entire life. After a car accident a year ago, he'd gotten hooked on painkillers. She thought he was finally kicking the habit only to discover he was so desperate for a fix, he'd tangled with the shifter smuggling network that had taken hold in Painter, Colorado. The only upside to the whole mess was he was now in treatment. Since his arrest was his first offense, he'd been given the chance to do treatment and community service. As long as he stayed clean for a year, all charges would be dropped at the end of the year.

Sophia stroked Jax's fur and glanced at Vivi. "How's it going?"

Vivi was already busy replanting the tulip into another flowerpot. Her long black hair was pulled into a ponytail that swished from side to side when she glanced over her shoulder. "Same, same. Busy with work and arguing with Julianna's new first grade teacher. I'm telling you, before you have kids, you'd better think long and hard. If it were just me and worrying about what I did, it wouldn't be so bad. Try facing down the school if you're worried about something. Mrs. Dunn is a bitch," she said flatly.

Sophia nodded and commiserated with Vivi. As a single mother to Julianna, Vivi had plenty on her plate. Sophia was relieved to focus on something other than everything that had been weighting her down lately. Between Heath's car accident, his difficult recovery, and the most recent mess, she felt like she'd dominated just about every conversation she had with Vivi. She was trying to let go of what she couldn't control. Being a sounding board for Vivi's frustrations with Julianna's new teacher was a nice change. As she stood to leave a while later, Vivi caught her eyes. "Any news?"

Sophia's heart clenched as she shook her head. "Nope." With Heath away, she kept hoping for something to shine a ray of hope. She also kept hoping for something to give in the wall of silence around the police investigation into the shifter smuggling network. Before Heath had brushed up against it, she and just about every shifter who wasn't involved had been concerned about the network's existence. It was rattling nerves and raising fears of exposure for shifters in the absolute worst light. With centuries of secrecy protecting shifters, some shifters had forgotten how important it was. While she'd certainly been concerned about the network before, she was fired up and furious since Heath had tangled with it. She knew perfectly well he was responsible for his own actions, but the easy access to drugs had offered a path for Heath to stumble along. Heartsick over witnessing her once proud and strong brother fall so low after his car accident, she was bound and determined to make sure they exposed the shifters involved once and for all.

Vivi stepped to her side and tugged her into a swift hug. Sophia gave a small wave once she stepped off the bottom step and walked down Vivi's short driveway to the road. She lived only a few minutes away and walked by almost every day on her way to work.

Moments later, she walked down Main Street in Painter, Colorado, a picturesque little town high in the Rocky Mountains, tucked in a small valley. She pushed through the door into Mile High Grounds, the small coffee shop she owned. When she'd decided to start this little café a few years ago, she hoped it would succeed, but it had done far better than she hoped. She glanced around to see most of the tables full and a line that wound almost to the door. She couldn't help the tiny hum of pride. She lifted the counter opening and stepped behind it, grabbing an apron and tying it around her waist quickly.

"Hey Josie," Sophia said when she stepped to Josie's side by the espresso maker.

Josie was one of her two main employees. Sophia had a few others that filled in, but Josie and Tommy were her regulars. Josie moved lightning fast as she served one espresso and immediately prepped for the next. "Hey Boss. It's been crazy all morning."

"Looks like. Want me to take over this part for a bit here?"

Josie shook her head. "Nah. I'm good. Tommy could probably use a hand at the register," she offered with a nod toward the counter.

Without a word, Sophia stepped to his side and turned on the other register. The line started moving more quickly, and Tommy stepped back to help Josie crank out coffees and serve bakery items. Sophia was on autopilot, taking orders, ringing them up in the computer and processing payment. She bantered with customers and savored the busyness to keep her mind off of her brother and the constant worry her parents were carrying.

She glanced up at the next customer and her breath

went out in a whoosh. The man standing at the counter instantly taught her the meaning of the phrase "took my breath away." A flush raced through her and her pulse quickened. The man was tall, dark and mouth-wateringly handsome. He had black hair on the longish side with dark curls edging the collar of his t-shirt. His navy blue eyes were bright against the contrast of his dark hair. His features were strong—sculpted cheekbones, a blade of a nose, and full sensual lips. His t-shirt was gloriously stretched tight across his muscles. She could actually count his six-pack of rock-hard abs.

She must have been silent a beat too long because the man arched a brow.

"Uh, what can I get for you?" she blurted out.

Wow. Pull it together. You sound like an idiot.

Sophia shook her head, trying to knock her obnoxious critic into silence. Oh-so-sexy man's mouth hooked on one side, his eyes glinting.

"Did I miss something?" he asked.

"Huh?"

"You shook your head."

She felt the heat race up her neck and face. *Maybe you should pay better attention to me sometimes. Shut up.* She sighed internally. She was having an entire conversation in her head while the sexiest man she'd ever laid eyes on stood there watching her and thinking she must be half crazy.

She met his eyes and forced smiled. "Oh, nothing. Coffee?"

His smile stretched from one corner of his mouth to the other. "That's what I came to find. What do you recommend?"

"It depends on what you like. Straight coffee? Or something more?"

"Something dark."

Dear God. The man had only said a few words and her heart was already racing, heat flooding her body.

"How about a double-shot Americano?"

"Perfect."

Sophia rang him up, while Josie got started on his coffee. Sophie couldn't help the curiosity. "Are you from around here?"

Oh-so-sexy shrugged. "Yes and no."

"What does that mean?"

"I was born here, but my family moved away when I was only three years old. I don't remember anything, but I always wanted to come back."

Her curiosity notched higher. Painter was a fairly small town. Born and raised here, Sophia knew almost everyone in town. If she didn't personally know them, she probably knew of them.

"Well, welcome back. I'm Sophia. There's a chance I might know your family. I've been here my whole life."

"Nice to meet you, Sophia. I'm Daniel, Daniel Hayes. My parents were David and Sarah Hayes." A blink of pain went through his eyes. "They both passed away in the last two years."

"Oh...I'm sorry." Her reply was automatic, but she meant it. She was close to her family, so the idea of somebody losing theirs was painful.

Daniel nodded. "Thanks. It's life." He paused and took a breath. Josie passed over his coffee. Sophie took it from her and slid it across the counter to him.

He took a swallow of coffee and closed his eyes with a sigh. "Wow. Damn good coffee." When his blue eyes landed on her again, her belly fluttered. Her body appeared to have a mind of its own when it came to this man.

She couldn't say why, but his parents' names were vaguely familiar. She didn't want to pry, so she left it alone.

"How long are you visiting?" she asked, trying to keep focused.

"I'm moving here for the summer actually."

"Oh. You just decided to move here?"

His navy eyes held hers steadily. "Yeah, pretty much. My mother always talked about Painter and how much she missed it. After she died, I decided I wanted to come find out what she loved about this place."

Sophia nodded slowly. "Well, summer's a wonderful time to be here."

"That's what I heard." He started to say something else when another customer stepped to the counter. He lifted his coffee. "I'll get out of your hair, but I'll be back. I'll be needing more of this amazing coffee."

Sophia watched him turn and walk away, his stride long and loose. She forced her attention to the next customer. The day raced by. Late that evening, when the sun was falling down behind the mountains, she walked down Main Street, heading back toward home. Her eyes tracked the motion of her cowboy boots, the pointed tips alternating in her line of sight. She was weary from a busy day, but in any free moment, her mind wandered to worrying about her brother. The only relief she had came from wondering about Daniel today.

DANIEL WALKED DOWN THE STREET, his eyes on the setting sun ahead. Painter was as beautiful as his mother had told him. The little town sat amidst the mountains, its streets winding along the hillsides. The view behind downtown was glorious at the moment. All that was left of the sun was a curved sliver above the ridge, bright orange with red and gold rays radiating into the sky behind it. Eyes on the sky, he suddenly collided with someone.

"Oomph!"

He looked down to find Sophia stumbling against him. Sophia was better known to his brain and body as the woman from the coffee shop who was so damn sexy he craved her as much as he craved coffee. Not even a single moment had passed since he'd met her for all of a few minutes and she'd been simmering in his mind all day. Her hands landed on his chest, and he didn't want her to move. One of his hands landed reflexively on her hip, while the other curled around her upper arm.

"I'm sorry! I wasn't paying attention." Her words came out rapidly.

"You and me both," Daniel replied with a wry smile. "I was looking at the sunset." He nodded behind her. She looked over her shoulder.

She turned back. "It's beautiful," she said softly.

Daniel nodded. He thought perhaps he should step back, but he couldn't. He felt the soft give of her hip under his palm. Her bright green eyes held his. A low charge hummed between them. He couldn't keep his eyes from flicking down. Her breasts pulled against the thin cotton of her black t-shirt. He forced his eyes up, only to have them land on her full mouth. He could see the flutter of her pulse in her neck, and he had to hold himself back from leaning over to drop his lips against the soft skin there. His arousal strained against his jeans, at which point he realized he was about to make a fool of himself. He shook his head and stepped back, his hands falling away.

He scrambled to recall what she'd said before his body had taken charge of his brain. *The sunset.* "It is," he said, his words coming out gruff.

Sophia's eyes held his, a green so deep he could lose himself in them. "I'll probably see you tomorrow if you're working again."

"Oh, okay."

As soon as the words left her mouth, Sophia rushed past him. He hadn't meant for that to be goodbye, but she seemed to have taken it as such. He turned and watched her walk away. Her dark hair hung straight down her back, swinging in tune with her walk. Her dark hair with her porcelain skin and bright green eyes was mesmerizing. When she'd looked up this morning, he'd wanted to reach across the counter and kiss her, right then and there.

Her hips swayed as she walked down the sidewalk. She wore purple leggings with black cowboy boots. Her leggings hugged her curvy hips and strong legs. Daniel watched her until she turned down a side street.

2

Sophia stirred the scrambled eggs and glanced over her shoulder at Vivi. "Do you know anything about David and Sarah Hayes?"

Vivi had stopped by for breakfast, something she often did on weekends. Her daughter Julianna was ensconced in the living room for her allotted half hour of Saturday morning cartoons. Vivi sat at the small round table in Sophia's kitchen. She was in the middle of braiding her hair into two side braids. She paused, her hands stilling on her hair. Her eyes narrowed and then widened. "Yeah. You don't remember hearing what happened with them?"

Sophie gave the eggs one last stir and turned off the burner. She quickly served the eggs on two plates and walked to the table, sliding one plate over to Vivi. "I thought I recognized their names, but I couldn't remember why." She paused and glanced at her empty coffee mug. "More coffee?" she asked, as she reached behind her and grabbed the coffee pot from the counter.

After she filled both of their mugs, she glanced back at

Vivi who had finished one braid and was working on the other. "So, what happened with the Hayes?"

Vivi looked through the archway from the kitchen into the living room at Julianna. Julianna was entirely focused on Scooby Doo. She had a fascination with the old school cartoons, in particular Scooby Doo. Vivi turned back, her blue eyes sober. "Don't you remember? Their son David was the little boy who shifted at a playground and ended up getting shot. The Hayes moved away and no one heard from them again."

Sophia set her fork down. "Oh my God. I remember hearing about that. No one talks about it, but it's the saddest thing. I can't imagine what that must have been like for them. Did they ever find out who killed him?"

Vivi nodded. "Yeah, it was a hunter. I'm sure we can look up the old news reports because Lord knows no one likes to talk about it. It's every shifter parent's nightmare. The guy said he turned around and saw a mountain lion in the middle of the playground, so he shot it. What brought them up?" Vivi finished braiding her hair and started to nibble on her eggs.

"Their other son, Daniel Hayes, showed up at the coffee shop today. He said he was moving here for the summer because he wanted to see the town his mother said was so beautiful."

Vivi's hand flew to her mouth with a gasp. "Oh wow. Really? Do you think he knows what happened?"

Sophia shrugged. "I have no idea. I only talked to him for a few minutes. He said he was born here, but they moved away when he was three. Both of his parents died in the last few years." She set her fork down. "Wow. If he knows what happened, I can't believe he'd want to come here."

Vivi nodded and took a sip of coffee. "I know, right? But he's here. Damn, once word gets around town, this is going to spin some heads. If he doesn't know what happened, I'd hate for him to find out through town gossip."

Sophia's own head was spinning and her heart hurt for Daniel and his family. Born and raised a shifter in one of the oldest shifter families in Painter, Sophia was steeped in the mindset of how important it was for shifters to maintain their secrecy. She hadn't recalled the names of Daniel's parents, but the memory of why they left was a bitter legend in Painter. The story held power as a warning among shifters, so she'd heard it time and again. She looked over at Vivi. "I hope he doesn't find out like that. I mean, that would be horrible. It's hard to imagine he'd be here if he knew though."

Julianna came wandering into the kitchen at that moment, leaning against her mother's hip. "Can I have some eggs?" she asked in her lilting voice.

Vivi brushed Julianna's dark hair off her forehead. "Aunt Sophia put red peppers in them. Think you can handle veggies in your eggs?"

Julianna's brown eyes bounced between Vivi and Sophia. "Uh huh," she said with an emphatic nod.

Sophia stood up and spooned some eggs into a small bowl for Julianna. "Here you go. I think you might like veggies this way."

Julianna set the bowl down on the table and took a small bite. Her eyes widened and she looked up at Sophia. "They're good!" she offered with a wondering smile.

Vivi chuckled and sipped her coffee. Sophia joined them at the table again. "You going to eat with us or Scooby?"

"Scooby!"

Vivi snagged a napkin from the center of the table and tucked it in Julianna's jeans pocket. "Make sure to put your bowl down when you're done."

Julianna held her bowl in both hands as she returned to

the living room. Once she was out of earshot, Vivi turned back to Sophia. "So what was Daniel Hayes like?"

Sophia recalled Daniel's almost black hair, blue eyes and body to die for. Her cheeks felt hot.

"Well, well. I'd say you thought Daniel was some kind of something," Vivi offered with a grin between bites.

Sophia's cheeks only got hotter. "You'll see him around soon enough. He's, uh, pretty damn handsome." Just talking about him flustered her. She didn't know why he had such a strong effect on her.

"Handsome or not, you don't usually go around blushing about guys. In fact, you hardly ever notice them."

Sophia shrugged. "So what? It's not like I have time for relationships. I'm busy running the coffee shop and with everything going on with Heath, I've had other things on my mind."

Vivi's eyes narrowed. "I care about Heath as much as you do. This year's been rough ever since he was in the accident. The last few months are just icing on a shitty cake. Heath is going to have to walk out of the mess he walked into. You can't do it for him. In the meantime, you could use a distraction. Just saying." Vivi's mouth curled into a wry grin.

Sophia's chest tightened. She was so weary of worrying about her brother. A year ago, his car had skidded on an icy road in the mountains and tumbled down a hill. He'd come out of the accident alive, but with multiple injuries, including a fractured femur in his thigh. It was that fracture that required multiple surgeries and caused him so much pain. The damn pain led to his painkiller addiction, and unbeknownst to anyone close to him, his subsequent search for heroin to replace the painkillers.

"Stop it," Vivi said sharply.

Sophia's eyes swung up to Vivi's. The warm concern in her gaze belied her stern tone of voice. Sophie sighed. "I know. I need to stop obsessing about Heath. I'm working on it."

"I get it, but all you can do is be there. A distraction like Daniel might be just the thing for you."

"You make it sound easy. Daniel showing up here is going to send gossip running wild. Not so sure he'll hang around."

Vivi took the last bite of her eggs and set her fork down. "Maybe so, but don't go making excuses before anything even happens."

DANIEL LEANED BACK in his desk chair and stretched his arms above his head. He'd been hard at work all morning. He was a computer coder and worked wherever he wanted, whenever he wanted. For the most part, it was great. The downside was he tended to get caught up in what he was doing and lose all track of time. His father had taught him computer coding when he was a little boy, so he'd had a head start before the rapid rise of technology jobs. He'd been working on his own doing contract work for companies all over the world since before he graduated from college. He loved the work and enjoyed the flexibility, but it didn't make for easy opportunities to meet people.

Now that he was in Painter, he wanted a chance to learn more about his family, which meant he needed to get out and meet people. His mind spun back to yesterday and Sophia. The last few years hadn't left much room for relationships. Between helping his mother care for his father in the year leading up to his eventual death from complications from heart surgery, grieving his father's death while supporting his mother and then grieving his mother's death within another year, it was fair to say he simply hadn't had the emotional energy to consider any relationships. He could barely remember the last time he went on a date.

Sophia had an effect on him unlike any he'd ever experienced. The fall of her dark hair, her deep green eyes and her generous curves were mesmerizing, but it wasn't that. It was something about her—he wanted to know her. He might not know her well, but he knew she'd been born and raised in Painter. He couldn't help but wonder if she knew his parents and might know more about what happened to his older brother whose death had led to his parents' abrupt departure from Painter so many years ago.

His mind spun back to the conversation he'd had with his mother when she was in the hospital.

"Daniel, I have to tell you something," his mother said. She'd been resting in her bed, her soft gold hair faded and threaded with silver. Her blue eyes had been weary. She hadn't been awake much for more than a few hours at a time, and talking was difficult at times due to the occasional bouts of coughing from pneumonia. He'd been standing by the window and turned to sit in the chair beside her bed.

When he met her eyes, he saw a sadness he only saw when she spoke of David who'd died when Daniel was only three. He barely remembered David. His gut tightened at the look in his mother's eyes. "What is it, Mom?"

She reached for his hand, curling his around it and squeezing. "I should have told you the truth long ago."

"What are you talking about?"

"About how David died."

His gut churning, Daniel had been uncertain if he should let his mother speak or discourage her. He didn't know what was better, or worse. She'd continued. "You know how you had those episodes when you're hiking?"

She was referring to times when he'd gone hiking and experienced what could only be described as frightening.

His skin prickled to the point of pain, he wanted to lash out and scream, and an otherworldly sense of power raced through him. Each time, he'd raced out of the woods and returned home. When he'd asked his mother to take him to a doctor, she'd avoided it, insisting it was nothing and would pass. The only thing he'd discovered was as long as he stayed out of the wilderness, the episodes didn't recur. After leaving Painter, his parents had moved to Denver. Though Denver was a bustling city, the mountains were right there and the city was filled with outdoor enthusiasts. Daniel had to curb his natural inclination to spend time hiking the many trails in the area. At his mother's question, he finally nodded.

Her eyes teared up. "I know exactly what was happening. I don't know how else to explain this, other than to just say it. It's going to sound crazy, but trust me, it's completely true. I didn't tell you before because I wanted to protect you the way I didn't manage to protect your brother."

He took a breath and nodded.

"You know those rumors you hear every so often about mountain lions that are also people?"

He could barely breathe, but he managed another nod. Whispers of mountain lion shifters were frequent in the area. Colorado, along with most of the West, was home to a healthy population of mountain lions. Rumor had it shifters lived amongst them, shifting from human to lion and back again at will. Daniel, along with most people, dismissed them as wild legends from times gone by.

His mother's eyes filled with tears again. He snagged a tissue from the box on the table by her bed and handed it to her. After she wiped her eyes, she took a labored breath. "Everyone in my family is a shifter. I'm one and so are you."

He felt like he was falling from a great height. Stunned, he simply stared at her.

"Those times you felt so strange were when your lion

wanted to come out. But you have to be ready and accept it for a full shift to happen. I'm so sorry I didn't say anything sooner, but I promised your father I wouldn't. The day before he died, he gave me permission to tell you when I thought the time was right. David died because he shifted at a playground. He had learned how to shift, but he didn't know how to control it yet. The man who shot him only saw a mountain lion in the middle of a bunch of children. Normally, I wouldn't have taken him to a park like that, but it was a school day trip. It was a horrible accident. Your father knew I was a shifter, his whole family knew. They were safe, and they'd protected the secret of shifters for years. After David died, I promised your father I wouldn't tell you. He didn't want you to die the same way."

Daniel sat there and tried to wrap his brain around what his mother was telling him. Somehow he stumbled through the rest of the conversation. She'd insisted he come back to talk more. In the intervening weeks before his mother died, she shared as much information as she could about her side of the family. Sadly, David's death had not only pushed their mother to disavow the shifter side of herself, but it had threatened the safety of the rest of her family. Shifters had lived in secret for centuries. David's unintentional shift had led to his own tragic death and heightened fear about shifters among those who were uncertain of their existence.

Daniel thought back to the day he'd hiked deep into the mountains and shifted. The visceral sensations that had so frightened him before whipped fluidly through him. He hadn't known what to expect. Doubt and disbelief dissolved in the face of reality as he stood there, fur rippling over his skin, power coursing through every step he took. In his lion form, he felt like he'd found a part of himself. He'd bounded free through the woods. It was as if his lion had been desperate for this day. It was past sunset with darkness thick in the trees when he shifted back into human form where he'd started.

Until that afternoon, he hadn't quite believed his mother. He hadn't thought she was lying, it was simply what she told him was so hard to believe. His mother had explained he would have been able to shift many years sooner, but it wasn't until adolescence the powers gained strength and became hard to resist. David's shadow had hung over his family for years, and now he knew why. He'd had a happy childhood despite the grief of his brother's death within the family.

Daniel shook his head, nudging his brain back to the present. He'd come to Painter to try to find all that had been lost for his family. He hoped to reconnect with any remaining family members left in Painter. He glanced at his watch and pushed away from his desk. He meant to get outside today, and he still had several hours of daylight left.

3

Sophia wiped down the back counters in the coffee shop and started the industrial dishwasher. The evening was winding down with closing time on its way. She glanced around the back, quickly noting that Tommy had already taken care of most everything in preparation for closing. He'd even prepped pastries for tomorrow morning. She washed her hands and walked back out front. The early evening crowd was comprised mostly of college students studying with a few tables chatting quietly.

She stepped to the counter to Tommy's side. "You can head out whenever you're ready," she said.

Tommy glanced to her, his brown eyes crinkling at the corners with his grin. "You sure?"

Tommy Dawson came from another local shifter family. He was a few years younger than her, but she'd known him all of her life since their families were close. She'd hired him when her mother nudged her to do so. She hadn't regretted it since. Tommy was reliable and a hard worker. He was also friendly, warm and engaging. At her nod, he ran a hand through his blondish-brown hair and untied the red apron with the Mile High Grounds logo on it. "I'm on first thing tomorrow, so I'll see you in the morning."

"That you will. Now go do something other than work!"

Tommy grabbed his jacket and headed out. Sophia tended the counter, which at this hour was a fairly quiet activity. She prepped herself a coffee and sipped on it while she flipped through today's paper. At the sound of her name, she looked up, straight into Daniel Hayes' eyes. Once again, he managed to rob her of her breath and her pulse took off.

When she didn't say anything right away, Daniel spoke. "How's it going? Hope it's not too late to order a coffee."

She mentally grabbed at her scattered thoughts and nodded, finally willing herself to speak. "Oh, of course it's not too late." She gestured to the small neon sign blinking in the window. "We're still open. What can I get for you?"

"What did I have yesterday?" he said, his mouth curling into a smile.

While she wasn't thinking too clearly, she remembered his order without a doubt because she'd replayed every word of their conversation too many times. She felt so silly, but Daniel called to her. She felt like she was back in high school experiencing her first crush. A passing encounter with him yesterday, and she could hardly stop thinking about him. Nothing but silly, girlish fantasies—she needed to get a grip and fast. "A double shot Americano. Would you like another?"

"Absolutely. Best coffee I've ever had," he said with a slow smile that sent flutters swirling through her belly.

"Coming right up." She stepped to the espresso machine and prepped his coffee, grateful for the busy work for a few minutes. All he had to do was smile, and she started to melt.

She slid his coffee across the counter. His fingers

brushed against hers when he took it. Electricity zapped from her fingertips and spun through the rest of her body. Her breath hitched, and slivers of heat slid through her veins. Daniel immediately took a swallow of coffee, closing his eyes with a sigh. "As good as I remembered." His blue eyes crinkled at the corners when he smiled again. He tugged his wallet out, his t-shirt riding up at the waist, revealing a flash of his rock-hard abs.

Somehow, she fumbled through ringing him up. He didn't seem inclined to go anywhere and leaned his hip against the counter. "Since you grew up here, I figured maybe you could tell me all the places I should check out around Painter."

Sophia tried to quell her skittering pulse, but she seemed to have little control over it, so she simply took a deep breath. Day in and day out, she chatted with customers, plenty of them handsome guys. Though on the small side, Painter was home to a state university and renowned for its skiing and hiking. As such, the town was filled to the brim with rugged, outdoorsy men. A healthy shifter population only added fuel to that fire. Male shifters were pure masculinity, strong and sexy with an alpha edge that couldn't be denied. Yet, she'd never been affected by any shifter the way Daniel affected her. He seemed to have a straight line to her body, the chemistry flickering hot and fast.

She glanced to Daniel and wondered what he knew of his heritage. She'd done a little sleuthing about his family since Vivi reminded her who they were. Sarah Hayes came from a family of shifters in Painter. His father attended college in Painter, which is how he met Daniel's mother. Sophia had no way of knowing if Daniel's father knew much about shifters, if he even knew she was a shifter. She'd sought out her mother for the story because she didn't want to end up being the source for the rumor mill that would most definitely start spinning once word got around that Daniel was here. Whether he knew it or not, the legend his family left behind was bitter and sad for the shifter community. Her mother would hold her silence. Lila Ashworth knew everything there was to know about anyone in Painter. She'd quickly repeated the story about Daniel's brother, David, and then shared the history of Sarah's family.

"After David died, the Weaver's closed up ranks. It was just Sarah's parents and her older brother. They kept a low profile and laid low. Her parents passed away not much later. Her brother is still around. Nelson Weaver. He keeps to himself. He lives on the family's property on the outskirts of town."

She belatedly realized she'd yet to reply to Daniel's comment. "Well, you found the best coffee place in town. Aside from that, Painter has some good restaurants. With the college here, Painter has some culture even though it's a small town in the Rockies. We're mostly known for the skiing and outdoors stuff. Although that's not specific to Painter. Find any town around here and it's filled with people seeking to escape to the wilderness. They don't like to talk about how half the reason the towns keep growing around here is because we make sure they have all the amenities they want. Anyway, what do you think so far? Is Painter as beautiful as your mother told you?"

Daniel's mouth hooked in a half-smile. He took another slow sip of coffee before he replied. "It is." He appeared to be considering something. She took a moment to soak him in. Her gut sensed he was a shifter. He emanated strength and an easy masculinity, which only added to his appeal.

"I'm wondering if you know anything about my family," Daniel said suddenly. "You mentioned you know most everyone in Painter since you grew up here. I didn't get much of a chance to know my mother's family."

Sophia met his eyes and saw curiosity with a hint of sadness underneath. She couldn't know with certainty, but she sensed he knew what happened to his brother and why his parents left Painter. Her heart clenched. She may have barely known him, but what had happened to his brother was heartbreaking. Shifters lived every day knowing they were walking between worlds. For his brother to die the way he did was uniquely painful. His death was solely due to shifting in the wrong place at the wrong time. All she could do was be honest, so that's what she did.

"Your family moved away before I was born, but I know a little bit about them." She paused and looked around the coffee shop. Only a few customers remained. She looked back to Daniel, trying to gauge what she should say.

He held her gaze, his expression somber. When he spoke, his voice was gruff. "You don't have to be afraid to talk about it. I know what happened to my brother."

"Oh... I'm sorry. I really am," she said because she didn't know what else to say, or how to acknowledge what had happened. So many years had passed, but she couldn't imagine what it must be like for him to return to the town where his brother died in the manner he did.

He gulped his coffee, as if fortifying himself. "It wasn't your fault. No need to apologize."

"I just meant I'm sorry it happened."

He nodded. "Right. Thanks. It's been a long time. I didn't mean to start such a serious conversation. I came here for the reason I said before. My mother loved Painter and missed it dearly. I also wanted a chance to see if I could find anyone from my mother's family."

Her mind spinning with the implications of Daniel's return here, she looked over at him and wondered what else she could tell him. Beyond the bare minimum, she didn't have much more to offer about his family. She started with what little she had. "Your mother's brother, Nelson

Weaver, is the only one left in Painter. He lives on your grandparent's old property. Honestly, the person you might want to talk to would be my mother."

Daniel's brows hitched up. "Really? Why your mother?"

She smiled ruefully. "Because she knows everyone and everything. She's also old enough to know a lot more about your family than me. I can take you to meet her if you'd like."

"I'd like that if you don't think she'd mind."

Sophia mentally rolled her eyes. She loved her mother dearly, but her mother loved to be involved. That wasn't always Sophia's preference, but for now it would work in Daniel's favor.

"Trust me, she won't mind. I'll give her a call about it."

"I'd really appreciate it."

At that moment, another customer approached the counter. Sophia prepped another coffee and handed it over. "We're closing up in fifteen minutes," she called out to the room in general.

The interruption knocked her conversation with Daniel onto more casual terrain, which she figured was a good thing. With little to offer, she didn't want to dwell on the sad situation surrounding his brother's death because she couldn't imagine it was pleasant for him.

Shortly thereafter, the coffee shop emptied and she got ready to close. Daniel had lingered by the counter. When she took her jacket off the hook behind the counter, he caught her eyes. "Can I walk you out?"

His question startled her, and she froze for a long moment. With his blue eyes holding hers, she couldn't look away and nodded without thinking.

DANIEL HELD his breath while he waited for Sophia to

answer. He'd stopped by Mile High Grounds telling himself he just needed a coffee. In the back of his mind, he wondered if he'd encounter Sophia and wondered yet again if she was as beautiful as he recalled. She was...and then some. He hadn't meant to ask about his family so abruptly, but he felt comfortable with her. There had been a flicker of surprise in her eyes when he mentioned he knew what happened to his brother. He could only imagine the incident had lingered in the memory of Painter. He was relieved for the interruption of the customer and then the bustle of Sophia saying goodbye as the other customers filtered out. Though the topic of David's death weighed on him, he'd had most of his life to accept it. He was glad to have the conversation naturally move on.

Sophia finally nodded, her green eyes bright with a flicker of uncertainty. He waited by the door while she flicked off the lights and turned the sign to 'closed' in the window. He followed her out onto the sidewalk. It was early evening with yet another glorious sunset over the mountains. The sky was painted in watercolor swirls of fading orange and red, the golden globe of the sun glowing bright as it fell behind the ridge ahead. Sophia wore black leggings and cowboy boots with a loose denim jacket tossed over a purple t-shirt.

She stopped on the sidewalk and turned to him. "I don't have a car for you to walk me to," she said with a half-smile. "I walked to work."

All he'd meant was to gain another few minutes in her presence because she called to him like no other, but it wasn't enough. His next words startled him because he wasn't thinking of anything other than that he wanted more time with her.

"How about dinner?"

Her green eyes widened. A soft breeze blew her dark hair across her face. She brushed it away, her eyes on him the entire time. She appeared to be considering something. "Okay. Dinner. If you don't mind having it at my place. My dog Daisy would be pretty upset with me if I didn't make sure she had dinner soon." A grin spread across her face when she mentioned her dog.

Daniel nodded. "Your place is fine. I'm looking forward to meeting Daisy. Can I give you a lift then?"

"It's not far, but sure."

Only minutes later, he was turning at her direction into a short driveway, rising sharply up the hillside. Her home was a charming bungalow painted white with a red tiled roof surrounded with other similar homes. Her yard was overflowing with flowers. As he followed her into her apartment, a deep bark greeted them. Sophia immediately knelt down and wrapped her arms around an enormous dog.

Sophia stood and glanced to him. "This is Daisy," she said gesturing to a dog who reached her waist. Daisy was stately and gray. She pinned Daniel with a curious gaze, her dark eyes blinking for a moment before she stepped to his side and sniffed his hand. He stroked her head, marveling at her size.

"Is she a Great Dane?"

Sophia nodded. "Yup. She's a gentle giant. She's only two, but she's mellow and sweet as pie."

Daisy leaned her head into his hand, her gaze soft and warm. Sophia kicked her boots off and hung her jacket by the door. As soon as she started to move away, Daisy followed her. Sophia looked back at him. "Feel free to hang up your jacket."

As soon as he did, he followed her through the living room and through an archway into the kitchen. The home was warm and inviting. The living room windows faced the mountains with a clear view of the setting sun through a bay window. A sage green couch with throw pillows scattered over it took up most of the living room. Plants were everywhere. The kitchen was small and cheery. A beautifully maintained porcelain stove was the centerpiece. The counters were polished slate. A round table was tucked into the corner.

The last rays of the sun fell through a side window, the light casting a soft glow in the room. Sophia quickly prepped a rather large bowl of food for Daisy who showed her only signs of impatience while waiting. Once Daisy was busy eating, Sophia looked up at him. Her hand rested on the curve of her generous hip. Her hair tumbled around her shoulders. Daniel tried to keep his eyes off of her breasts, but it was damn difficult with her t-shirt stretched tight over them.

"Okay, now that Daisy has dinner, we can talk about what we're having. How about takeout from the best pizza place in town?"

"Sounds perfect. What's the best pizza place in town?"

She snagged a menu off the refrigerator, which was papered with menus and postcards, and tossed it to him. "Painter's Pizza. It's been around forever. Classic deep-dish pizza when it started. They've expanded their choices in the last few years with healthier options to cater to the college kids and the new health craze. They even have gluten free crust if that's your fancy."

She plunked down at the kitchen table and gestured for him to join her. After a few moments, she arched one of her dark brows. "Well, what do you think?"

He handed the menu back to her. "Honestly, I'll eat anything. If you want to go old school with pepperoni, or get fancy with some of the veggie options, it's fine either way. What's your preference?"

Sophia flipped the paper menu back and forth in her fingers. "Let's do half and half. I love pepperoni, but I like to convince myself I'm trying to be healthy sometimes too. Their spinach feta pizza is amazing."

"Sounds good."

She slipped her phone out of her pocket and quickly placed their order. While they waited, she stood and opened her refrigerator. "Beer? Wine?"

"Beer will do."

After she handed him one, she gestured for him to follow her into the living room once Daisy finished eating. The time passed quickly. Sophia was easy and comfortable to talk with. The only distraction was the buzz of electricity that swirled in a current around them. She seemed oblivious to her effect on him while he could barely sit still around her. The pizza arrived, and it was as good as Sophia had promised.

Meanwhile, he soaked her in. The fall of her dark hair that swung down her back, her emerald eyes, the delicate arch of her brows, her bow-shaped lips, and the lush curves of her body. As the evening passed, one thing came into sharp focus. He wanted Sophia fiercely. He didn't know if it was his recent acquaintance with his shifter side, but desire pounded through him in a way he'd never experienced. Though the events of his life had precluded relationships in his recent history, he'd had a healthy interest in women and dated plenty before that. But whatever he felt for Sophia burned hot and fast. His mind grappled with it, telling him he needed to pace himself and not move too quickly.

Daisy had fallen asleep on the floor, stretched out and dead to the world. Sophia stood from the sofa and reached to take his plate, her fingers brushing his. Electricity jolted through him, the power so strong he wouldn't have been surprised if he saw sparks. Her breath drew in sharply. The plate wobbled in her hand, but she held onto it. Lust coursed through him, the power of it almost overtaking him. He shackled it. The lion side of himself he'd only come to know recently simmered under the surface of his skin.

He stood and followed her to the kitchen, leaning against the wall. When she turned away from the sink, she remained where she was by the counter, her hands curling around the edge. He pushed away from the wall and took a few steps in her direction, stopping several feet away. "Look, I, uh, don't mean for this to come out of the blue, but I want to kiss you—like I've never wanted to kiss anyone before."

Her green gaze slammed up to his. She swallowed, and he could see her pulse fluttering in her neck. Her hands slowly uncurled from the counter, her arms falling to her sides. She took a step in his direction and stopped. "How...?"

He shrugged. If he let his mind run the show, it was like static interfering. If he let his feelings speak, he knew with certainty that whatever lie between him and Sophia was special. Even if he'd only just met her. He held her eyes. "I don't know how. I just know I feel something with you I've never felt before, and I don't want to pretend like it's not there. I won't rush. We can take our time. I just thought maybe I should be honest about it from the start."

4

Sophie stared at Daniel, her eyes taking him in—all tall, dark and so sexy she nearly melted in his presence. If she hadn't been certain he was a shifter, she knew he was now. The intense energy, the primal pulse of desire pounding between them—only that kind of energy came from a shifter. She sensed he was as thrown by this as she was. Yesterday, he'd walked into her coffee shop and taken her breath away. When he'd appeared again today, it was as if flames flickered between them in every moment.

When he asked her about dinner, she elected to invite him here because Daisy was her best radar. She figured a casual dinner could be just that, or she could learn if Daniel passed Daisy's inspection. He passed with flying colors. Daisy tended to be standoffish if she was uncertain about anyone new. She'd immediately been comfortable with Daniel. Sophia looked over and Daniel and wondered if she was out of her mind. She was seriously considering kissing this man. Her brain started to chatter. *You have too much going on. You can't do this. You have to help Heath, you're busy with the store, you need to be there for your parents...*

Okay, how about you shut the hell up? Remember what Vivi said? No excuses before something even happens. All he said was he wanted to kiss you. It's just a kiss. What's one kiss? As she carried on with her internal debate, she could imagine what Vivi would say. *Maybe a distraction is just what you need.*

She shook her head sharply, trying to knock the chatter into silence. Daniel cocked his head to the side. "Am I missing something again?"

Her cheeks got hot as she shook her head. "No, uh, just…" Her words trailed off, and she flushed deeper. "What do you mean 'again'?"

His mouth hooked up on one side. "You shook your head when I saw you yesterday, and I hadn't even asked a question."

A giggle bubbled up. She felt silly because both times she was trying to shut her damn mind up. All because Daniel had this unreal effect on her. It had been a solid year since she'd kissed anyone. She'd never enjoyed the world of dating. It was annoying trying to weed through who was worth it and who wasn't. In the tight-knit world of shifters, there was another layer to navigate. Shifters didn't always pair up with other shifters, but the hope was always there. The last few years had torn at the fabric of trust in the shifter community with the smuggling network that had sprung up in Painter. It was a small fraction of the community, but the betrayal ran deep. No one knew who to trust, which made any consideration of relationships nearly impossible. It passed through her mind that perhaps she had reason to doubt Daniel. Her gut reacted powerfully to that. She might not know him well, but the cat in her trusted him completely. That itself conflicted her. Just because the primal side of her trusted him didn't mean she should just dive in. Yet, it was so rare to feel that trust combined with the deep sense of longing he elicited.

She made an impulsive decision. With Daniel's eyes on her, she closed the distance between them and stopped inches away. She tried to remember what he'd last said, but she couldn't. When she angled her head to look up at him, he stepped another inch closer. "Does this mean...?"

She nodded before he could finish his question. The air around them heated as he remained still. Her belly fluttered and heat flooded through her limbs. In slow motion, Daniel lifted a hand and stroked it into her hair, sliding his palm to cup the side of her face. His thumb coasted across her pulse. His blue gaze seared into hers as he leaned forward. Her entire being arched into his touch, seeking more. Fierce need raced through her. His lips landed softly at the corner of her brow. He feathered kisses across her face, each one sending sparks of electricity in its wake. Hot shivers coursed through her. Finally, his lips met hers. His kiss started soft, but quickly shifted to hot and deep when she gasped into his mouth.

The depth of her need was answered by his kiss—slow, deep strokes of his tongue tangling with hers. His hands roamed over her body, his touch strong and sure. Her low belly clenched. Hot, liquid need swirled in her center. She flexed into his touch, her hands running over the hard planes of his body. Their kiss went on and on. Her cat shimmered underneath, nearly purring with satisfaction at the feel of him under her touch.

When he finally tore away, her breath came in heaves. Her sex was drenched with need, and she most certainly did not want to stop. They remained where they were. Daniel's palm was resting on her low back, his other hand laced in her hair. Her head came to his shoulder, and she could feel the pounding of his heart against her. She tried to gather herself, the fuzz in her brain slowly clearing though her want for him didn't abate in the least. A tad bit of reason prevailed, reminding her that maybe slowing down a bit would be wise. He stepped back a fraction, his hand sliding free of her hair. He tucked a few loose locks behind her ear, sending shivers in the wake of his touch.

Just a kiss was the understatement of the century.

SOPHIA KNOCKED QUICKLY on the kitchen door at her parents' house before stepping inside. Her parents lived in the home where she grew up. It was located a few miles from downtown Painter on the edge of a small valley. Their home was a farmhouse built when her great-grandparents moved to Painter from Maine over a century ago. The home was elegant and simple, a colonial style farmhouse painted a soft gray with green trim. As she stepped into the kitchen, the sun was falling in bright rays through the tall windows, casting a sheen on the polished hardwood floor. The kitchen had been updated with new stainless steel appliances though it retained its original charm. Her mother had given Sophia her love of plants. The kitchen had ferns hanging in the corners and flowers on the windowsills.

"Hey Mom!" she called as she walked inside.

She heard a muted reply and followed it down the hall to the study at the front of the house. Her mother was standing up from her desk as she entered. Lila Ashworth's hair was almost black and streaked with silver. It swung about her shoulders as she walked toward Sophia. Her eyes were dark brown and usually held a gleam of suppressed mirth, though that had been all but extinguished in the last year between Heath's car accident and subsequent problems. The fog had started to lift and then Heath had been arrested.

Lila walked to Sophia and slipped her hand through Sophia's elbow. "I meant to be finished up in here. I've been grading papers all morning, and I'm ready for a break. I thought we could have a snack in the kitchen."

Sophia walked alongside her mother back to the kitchen. Lila immediately put out a small tray of cheese and crackers on the table, along with a pitcher of lemonade, and sat down across from Sophia at the small table tucked into an alcove of windows. The flower filled backyard stretched out in view.

"I thought you weren't going to do any teaching this summer," Sophia commented as she filled the two glasses her mother set out with lemonade.

Lila lifted one shoulder in a small shrug. "I wasn't, but then the high school called because the teacher they had lined up to cover the summer school English classes quit. It's only two days a week. It keeps me busy, so that's a good thing," she offered with a wry smile.

Sophia held her mother's gaze for a long moment. "Any word from Heath?"

Lila took a sip of lemonade and nodded. "He called last night. He sounds better every time we talk. If he apologizes one more time, I might scream, but he keeps apologizing anyway."

After his arrest for trying to buy heroin, Heath had worked out a deal with the local prosecutor to go to rehab and do community service upon his return. If he stayed clean for the year after, his charges would be dropped. He'd been away in rehab for over a month now. Every time Sophia tried to wrap her brain around the fact that Heath had gotten so addicted to painkillers he went hunting for heroin, she felt like she was in an alternate universe. Prior to his car accident, Heath had been nothing other than stable and steady as a rock. He'd gone into the military straight out of high school, worked his way into the Special Forces in the Marines and lived an upstanding life. His accident had derailed his military career, although fortunately he'd been honorably discharged before the stain of his arrest occurred. Now, he was working his way back to the life he had before. Sophia spoke to him weekly, but she knew he spoke to their parents almost every day. The brother she knew and loved was weighted down with guilt over the events of the last year. No matter how many times she reminded herself only Heath could be held responsible for his actions, she remained sick with fury about the smuggling network and the easy gateway it opened in Painter.

"He's probably going to keep apologizing, so I suppose you'd better get used to it," Sophia replied. "He feels terrible. I'm just relieved he's finally getting help. I wish we'd understood how addictive those damn painkillers could be." She shook her head sharply and grabbed a cracker.

Lila watched her for a long moment before shaking her own head. "Enough of that. Your father keeps telling me to stop dwelling, so moving on. Ever since you asked me about the Hayes family the other day, I've been wondering how their son is doing. If I have it right, he should be about thirty-two years old now. I can't believe it's been that long since they moved away. Have you seen him again?"

"Actually, I have. I kind of have a favor to ask."

Lila cocked her head to the side and nodded for Sophia to continue.

"He asked me what I knew about his family. Since I don't know much, I suggested he talk to you. I hope you don't mind."

"Of course I don't mind. Does he even know what happened to his brother?"

"He does. I didn't ask, but he offered it up. I probably didn't do the best job of hiding my expression when he asked about his family. I guess he wants to learn about them. Seeing as the only one left is Nelson Weaver, and I barely know who he is, I thought you had a lot more to share. You know everyone and everything."

Lila laughed softly. "Not everyone and everything, but I do know most everyone in Painter. I knew his mother because we grew up together. I know his uncle, but Nelson has all but disappeared the last few years. After David died, Daniel's grandparents were devastated. They kept to themselves. The whole thing was just terrible. It was bad enough David was shot and killed in front of all those children on the playground, but there were some shifters who blamed the family for putting shifters at risk."

"What do you mean?"

"The man shot a mountain lion, but once David fell to the ground, he shifted back to human form. Needless to say, it was terrifying. Except for shifters and the humans who already knew they existed, it was like nothing they'd ever imagined. Thank goodness the local police covered it up. Shifter rumors have always been a concern, but it was years before things quieted down after that. The last few years have got people nervous again because of that damn smuggling network."

Sophia sat quietly for a moment, absorbing what her mother said. Shifters had been so successful at hiding in plain sight for so long, sometimes she forgot how precarious their secrecy could be. All it would take would be something like what happened to Daniel's brother, or one of the shifter smugglers getting caught in the wrong place and wrong time. She took a breath and brought her mind back to the moment.

"The whole thing is so sad. It seems like that incident overshadows almost everything about Daniel's family."

Lila nodded, her eyes tinged with sadness. "Hard not to. The saving grace for Daniel now is it's been so long. I can tell him what his mother was like before all that. I got to know his father some, but his father was from a nearby town, so I didn't know him the same way. Next time you see Daniel, tell him I'd be glad to talk with him. Maybe you can bring him out here sometime soon."

"That's what I was hoping," Sophia said with a grin.

Lila eyed her for a long moment. "Tell me, what's going on with you and him?"

Sophia felt a ping in her center. Her mother was disconcertingly good at picking up on anything with her. She sighed internally. If she tried to hide it, her mother would know. She shrugged. "I don't know. I just met him, but he's, uh..." Her cheeks got hot when the memory of his lips against hers flashed through her mind.

Her mother grinned. "Any man that can get you to notice him must be pretty damn amazing! I can barely remember the last time you even bothered with dating."

Sophia groaned and half-glared at her mother. "He's just a nice guy. Don't turn this into something when it's not."

Her mother chuckled. "Fine. I'll leave you be. In the meantime, let me know when you're bringing him by."

Mercifully, the conversation moved on. Sophia left a while later and headed straight to Vivi's house. When she pulled up, Vivi was on the porch again. Sophia walked up the stairs and plunked down in a chair. Vivi glanced over from where she was trimming basil.

"Hey there. On your way home?"

Sophia nodded. "Since I can't get there without passing by your house, I figured I might as well stop," she replied with a grin.

Vivi had turned back to the basil, snipping its leaves and dropping them in a small bowl. Jax leapt onto Sophia's lap, instantly purring when she stroked a hand down his back. After a few moments, Vivi set the scissors down and sat down in the chair beside Sophia. When she met Sophia's eyes, her gaze was thoughtful.

"What's up?" Sophia asked.

Vivi was quiet for a beat before she spoke. "I'm wondering if you're up for a run into the mountains with me."

Anxiety coiled through Sophia. Ever since Heath had been arrested, she and Vivi had been doing some of their own investigating into the smuggling network. The open secret of the smuggling shifters had been rumbling under the surface of Painter for the last few years. The police had made some local arrests, but little headway had been made. When news broke that the network had stretched its tentacles all the way to Catamount, Maine, the birthplace of shifters, the shifters who were horrified about it had become more vocal. Rumor had it someone, a highly secretive someone, had started the whole mess in Painter. Catamount had succeeded in shutting off the source in its community, so Sophia and Vivi figured that's what needed to happen in Painter. Heath's situation kept her anger on a high simmer and pushed her to find a way to do something, anything, to put a stop to the network.

She met Vivi's gaze. "Of course. Anything new?"

Vivi shrugged. "Maybe, maybe not. I was at Quinn's last night and heard some of the guys talking about a meeting place in the woods to the south side of town. I figure we head out for a run and see what we find."

Quinn's was a local restaurant and bar in Painter, the go-to place for practically everyone in town. Vivi worked there on occasion when they needed backup at the bar. Her primary job was managing the small landscaping business she owned, but as a single mother, any extra cash flow was a good thing.

Sophia glanced at her watch. "I've got a few hours before I need to head to the coffee shop to help close up. If we're going to scout around, we should go now."

SOPHIA STOOD alongside a stream roughly a half-mile into the woods. She and Vivi hiked here often, but they never shifted until they were far enough into the woods to be able to shift sight unseen. Birds chattered in the trees. After a last look around to ensure they were alone, Sophia shifted. Energy coursed through her in a wave, her skin prickled as fur rippled across its surface. Power rose inside as her cat emerged. In seconds, she and Vivi were jogging quietly through the trees, weaving their way deeper into the mountains. Vivi had only vague information about where this alleged meeting place was, but the advantage to searching in lion form was they could cover a lot of ground in little time.

They moved in unison through the trees, pausing to scent out areas. Sophia savored the quiet and the sense of freedom she felt when her cat could roam free. Miles into their exploration, Sophia sensed someone nearby. She froze with Vivi freezing at her side. They stood in the quiet and listened. Her cat senses were so much more powerful than her human senses. A shifter in human form had much stronger senses than a regular human, yet they couldn't carry the full power of their lion capabilities with them. In the distance, her ears picked up human voices, and she could barely smell mountain lion. Considering it was rare to scent lions and humans in the same area, it likely meant shifters were nearby.

She and Vivi quickly began moving, keeping to the ridgeline and in the trees. They were close to a small valley that opened up. After several moments of stealthy running, they paused behind a large boulder at the edge of the forest. With careful positioning, they could see into the small valley. An old hunting cabin sat beside a stream on the far side of the valley. The cabin was so old, it listed to one side. She recalled traveling through this area a few years back, but it was far enough out few shifters traveled through this area. In a small clearing beside the cabin, two men stood talking. Sophia and Vivi watched quietly. As they watched, two mountain lions appeared in the trees behind the cabin. In seconds, they shifted into human form and reappeared moments later in the clearing. The group of men went out of sight into the cabin, at which point, Sophia caught Vivi's eyes and swung her head toward the valley. Without waiting, Sophia slipped from behind the boulder and starting running along the edge of the forest, looping around the valley to get closer to the cabin. Adrenaline surged through her, anger the driving force. She wanted to see who the hell was here and why.

She felt Vivi race to her side and bump against her shoulder as they closed in on the far side of the valley. The cabin was close enough for her to see motion through the windows. Vivi nudged her more forcefully again. Sophia ignored her and dodged through the trees. Vivi didn't take the hint and dashed in front of her with a low growl, knocking her off balance. She scrambled to gain her footing, but Vivi didn't allow it. Vivi knocked her right back down. Sophia knew Vivi was trying to keep her from doing something stupid, but at the moment, she didn't want to listen. When she tried yet again to push back, Vivi didn't hesitate and quickly swatted at her.

Sophia finally relented when they heard voices by the cabin. They froze together and waited in the trees until it had been quiet for several long moments. They moved deep into the trees again and retraced their path. They shifted back into human form and walked quickly to Sophia's car. By mutual agreement, they didn't speak until they were in the car with both doors closed.

Vivi took a swig from her water bottle before she spoke.

"Well, damn. I wonder how long they've been meeting there. Could you tell who any of them were?"

Sophia looked over at her before she started the car. "Hard to say for sure, but I think the two shifters who showed up in the trees were Randy and Doyle Norman."

She almost spit their names out. Randy and Doyle were the dealers Heath had sought out. They were local and low-level. They'd been arrested with him, but had somehow managed to finagle getting out on bail while they waited for trial. Every damn thing about the situation infuriated her. Heath's life had been blown up, while Randy and Doyle just got right back to doing what they did.

Vivi nodded. "That was my guess. I couldn't get a good look at the two guys who were already there though. You?"

"Nah. They had their backs to us almost the whole time." She started her car and backed up in the small parking lot. The area where they'd hiked in was a state managed reserve. There was a single marked trail leading away from the parking area. She quickly drove back into town and pulled into Vivi's driveway.

"What now?" she asked, looking to Vivi.

"I'm headed back for another pick up shift at Quinn's tonight. I'll ask around." Vivi brushed her hair away from her face, quickly tying it into a knot. "The good news is we know at least one place Randy and Doyle are using."

"Yeah, but we don't know if it means anything."

Vivi swung to her. "I know you tend to be trusting and cautious, but here's what we know. Randy and Doyle have already been charged with dealing. It's been rumored they're involved with the smugglers. Now we know they're meeting in the middle of nowhere at an old abandoned cabin. You might not want to connect the dots, but I have no problem doing so. We just need to keep following the bread crumbs. Eventually, they'll lead us higher up the chain. After what happened with Heath, we can't keep hoping this will go away on its own."

Sophia leaned her head back and sighed. "I know, I know. I'm just tired of it all." She felt like she'd been weary day in and day out ever since she picked up the phone and raced to the hospital to wait for news on Heath. His life had gone into a skid that day and was only now, maybe, just maybe, slowing enough for him to get back on track. The only respite she'd experienced had been since she met Daniel. Beyond the attraction that sizzled like a livewire between them, he was a breath of fresh air in her life and took her mind off the relentless loop of worries in her mind.

Vivi leaned over and pecked her on the cheek. "We all are. Just think about Heath."

Sophia watched Vivi jog up the stairs. She understood why Vivi reminded her to think of Heath, but the reminder was wholly unnecessary. She also had to keep fighting an internal battle not to just go straight to the police, but nothing seemed to go anywhere with them. With another sigh, she backed up and drove the short distance to her house.

5

Daniel ran through the forest, weaving his way up the mountainside. A soft breeze carried through the trees, rippling through his fur. Since he'd moved to Painter, he found himself exploring the woods and mountains daily. His lion called to him, and he couldn't deny he savored the sense of power and freedom that surged through him whenever he shifted. The trees in this area were mostly aspen, their leaves twirling in the breeze. In the year since he'd learned of his true nature and learned how to shift, he spent as much time as he could running free through the forest and mountains. Moving to Painter brought him closer to the lion side of himself, primarily because the town sat nestled amidst the mountains. Every moment he was outside, the mountains called to him. He wondered if the urge to shift would abate somewhat after he'd had more time to experience it.

For now, he kept climbing up the mountainside. He loved that he was so nimble in lion form. He easily climbed cliffs and traversed along rocky ledges he could never have considered in human form. As he wove through the trees, he scented another mountain lion nearby. A small valley was off to one side through the forest. The scent drifted to him on the breeze from that direction. He froze for a moment before carefully making his way to a vantage point in the edge of the trees.

What looked to be an abandoned cabin sat on the far side of the valley. The area around it held traces of recent activity. The tall grasses were trampled down. The door hung open. As Daniel watched, another mountain lion came into view. The lion paused in the edge of the trees before stepping out into the open field. Right before Daniel's eyes, the mountain lion shifted into human form, walking casually to the small cabin and tugging on clothing by the doorway.

Even though Daniel was fully aware shifters existed, seeing as he now knew he was one, he'd never seen another human shift. With only the advice given to him by his mother, he'd ventured into the mountains on his own and stumbled through the process of shifting. Watching it happen was mind-boggling. His senses told him something was afoot here, but he had nothing to go on other than his gut. He held still and kept watching. Long moments later, the man who'd walked into the cabin came back out followed by another. In a flash, both shifted and bolted into the forest. He had to wrestle with himself to keep from following. The only thing keeping him back was the weak hold he had on his sense of human reason. Among other details, his mother had warned him he would likely encounter other shifters and to remember male shifters were territorial. She'd assured him he could hold his own, but not to make rash choices in the wilderness because the human rules and laws didn't apply.

As such, he remained where he was, listening to the

rustle of the two lions running in the distance, further and further away from him. Filled with questions, he turned away and raced through the falling darkness back home.

When he returned home, after shifting back to human form, he was restless and driven. Sophia wove through his thoughts. He could hardly keep her out of his mind after their kiss the other night. Since he could use a cup of coffee just about anytime, he figured it was the perfect excuse to see Sophia. He grabbed his jacket and took off.

SOPHIA SAVORED the busy work of making one coffee drink after another. She pulled another shot of espresso for the next drink and passed it over to Tommy who stood at her side. It was summer exam week for the college students, so Mile High Grounds was filled to the brim with students studying and grabbing a coffee before they headed off to various locations to pull an all-nighter. Customers streamed up to the counter with the pace only starting slow after the sun fell behind the mountain ridge. She was busy wiping down the espresso machine when Tommy tapped her on the shoulder.

"What?" she asked.

He merely nudged his chin in the direction of the door, a gleam of mirth in his brown eyes. She looked to the door and saw Daniel stepping through—tall, dark and way too sexy for his own good. Her breath hitched and butterflies thronged in her belly. *You need to get a grip. One kiss and you're gaga. Must be because you haven't kissed anyone in so damn long. Nope, it's not that. It's Daniel. You like him and you'd better get a handle on it because he's only here for the summer. All the more reason to have a little fun.* Her mind had its own little tennis game going, volleys lobbed back and forth. She shook her head, only to glance away and find Tommy eyeing her and choking back a laugh.

"What?" she asked again.

Tommy shrugged. "Saw you walking out with Mr. Hottie there the other night. I wondered what was up and now I know."

She put a hand on her hip and glared at him. "All I did was walk out with him."

Tommy shook his head. "Saw you get in the car with him. Maybe none of my business, but as far as I'm concerned, you deserve to have a little fun."

Tommy didn't state it explicitly, but she knew he was referring to the last year and everything that had transpired since Heath's accident. With his family close to hers, he was well-aware of all Heath had been through and the collective worry of family and friends. Much as she wanted to be annoyed with him, she knew he meant well. She rolled her eyes and went back to cleaning, focusing on the intricacies of cleaning around the knobs and the various parts of the espresso machine.

"I barely know him though, so don't go getting any ideas."

Tommy was quiet for long enough, she looked up. His eyes had sobered. "I heard his brother was that little boy who got shot in the playground."

Her heart clenched with a throb of sadness. She sighed and stopped what she was doing. "You heard right, but don't go gossiping about it. It's bad enough he had to lose his brother. He doesn't need all of Painter shifters whispering behind his back."

Tommy was younger, but he had a good head on his shoulders and a good heart. He nodded. "I know. I was just curious if you knew."

At that moment, Daniel reached the counter. It was

impossible for Sophia not to look up at him. Her body hummed like a tuning fork in his presence. As soon as she looked up, she found herself caught in the web of his gaze. All he did was stand there, one hand tucked casually into the pocket of his jeans. Her eyes went instantly to the strip of skin and rock-hard abs revealed where his jeans tugged down below his t-shirt. She forced her eyes up. He wore faded blue jeans paired with a navy t-shirt and a black leather jacket tossed over his shoulder, hanging from his thumb. His dark curls were windblown, his blue eyes bright and locked on her.

She was frozen in place while her body vibrated inside and hot need slid through her veins. It was hard to think of what she felt with Daniel in the context of the lighthearted fun of which Tommy spoke. What she felt for Daniel ran deep. The air between them snapped with tension. She realized she hadn't spoken a word and was just standing there by the espresso machine with a towel in her hand. Tommy had made himself quite busy serving another customer who she happened to know was a good friend, so they were obviously doing all they could to make it so Sophia had no choice but to wait on Daniel. Not that she minded, but she needed to get a handle on herself.

She tossed the towel behind her into the small laundry basket tucked out of sight under the counter and took a deep breath, gathering herself. His eyes tracked her as she took the few steps from behind the espresso machine to the counter. She curled her hands on the edge of the counter giving herself something to hold onto.

"Hey there," Daniel said, his gravelly voice sending shivers straight through her.

"Hi," she managed to say.

After a taut moment, he allowed the arm hooked over his shoulder holding his jacket to fall and looped the jacket over his elbow. "Don't suppose I could order another one of your amazing coffees?"

"Of course! That's what we do here. Any preferences?" She was relieved at his perfectly ordinary question. It put her back on the track of habitual conversation.

"I think I have a usual," he said with a low chuckle that sent heat scoring through her center.

"Would that be the double-shot Americano then?"

He nodded with a slow smile gracing his face. With her pulse skittering wild, she stepped to the espresso machine, quickly prepping his coffee. When she returned to the counter and handed it to him, his fingers brushed against hers. Electricity zipped through her from his casual touch. She completely forgot to charge him, but he held out a five-dollar bill. She flushed and shook her head before realizing she was once again shaking her head at what looked like nothing to him. When she held out his change, his mouth had hooked on one corner, and she knew he'd noticed. She couldn't help but wonder if he thought her silly and foolish with her random head shaking. If only he knew it was because he rattled her so much, she couldn't think clearly.

Tommy was still chatting with his friend, so there was nothing to distract her from Daniel. He took a long, slow swallow of coffee and then pinned her with his intense navy gaze. "I was hoping I could persuade you to let me take you to dinner."

She was nodding affirmatively before she even thought about it. By the time her brain caught up with her body, she didn't know what to do. It wasn't that she didn't want to go. The problem was she *really* wanted to go, and she didn't quite know what to do about that. She wasn't used to wanting a man, much less lusting after one the way she did Daniel. He set her on fire simply by existing in space near her.

"I'll take that as a yes then," he said, his eyes glinted with mirth.

"Oh, right. Yes. That was a yes." *Okay, now you definitely look foolish and silly. All you had to say was yes.* She fought the urge to shake her voice to silence again.

Several beats of silence passed while Sophia tried to gain control of her body. One look from him, and heat curled through her veins, her belly somersaulted, and her pulse galloped wildly beyond her control. As they stood there, the low murmur of voices in the coffee shop filtered through her consciousness. A laugh from Tommy knocked her out of her stupor. She shook her head—again—and looked back at Daniel. Her cheeks were hot, but she managed to speak. "Any ideas where you want to go?"

"I was hoping you could make a few suggestions. So far, I've had the coffee here, pizza with you the other night, and I've made one stop at the local grocery store."

"If you want to get to know Painter, we should go to Quinn's."

"What's Quinn's?"

"Quinn's Restaurant and Bar. It's been here forever. It's owned by the Quinn family," she said with a wry grin. "They've been here as long as I can remember. It's impossible to go there without running into plenty of locals, so you'll get a chance to get to know some people. A friend of mine, Vivi Sheldon, covers extra shifts sometimes, so you might meet her. You said you wanted to get to know the town, so…"

Daniel nodded firmly. "That I did. Quinn's sounds great. When do you close up here?"

Sophia glanced at the clock above the door. "In about a half hour. If you don't mind waiting, I need to clean up and do a little prep for tomorrow."

Daniel nodded with a half-smile. She watched as he walked away, his stride long and loose. His shoulders flexed under his t-shirt as he set his coffee down at a table nearby and slid into the chair. Only when Tommy cleared his throat did she look up.

Tommy grinned. "You've got it bad."

She bit her lip and flushed. Tommy was right. She was in deep.

6

______

Daniel followed Sophia into Quinn's. Quinn's was on the edge of downtown in an older building with a classic western façade on the front. The restaurant and bar had clearly been a restaurant and bar for many, many years. A polished wooden bar sat against the back wall, running the entire length of the space. The wood was worn and grooved from years of use. They waited at the corner of the bar for a table to open up. Quinn's was busy, and Daniel figured the place was usually busy. Beyond the bar, round tables were scattered throughout the center of the large room with booths lining the walls. An archway led into another section that held pool tables and card tables. The place had a rustic feeling with warm touches added through a mix of Native American artwork and sports memorabilia. What could have been an odd mix felt right at home in Quinn's. The customers ran the gamut from college students to families to just about anyone.

Sophia hadn't been kidding when she said she knew most everyone in Painter. While they waited for a table, practically anyone that passed by stopped to greet her.

Daniel met so many people, he lost track of who was who. Eventually, a waitress tapped Sophia on the shoulder and pointed to a corner booth just opening up. Moments later, he looked across the table at her. Whenever he was with her, his body ran on high idle—lust humming just under the surface. When distractions weren't present, he couldn't keep his eyes off of her. Her dark hair was loose tonight, a silky fall around her shoulders. The green of her eyes was vivid even in the muted lighting.

She caught his eyes, and her cheeks flushed slightly. He didn't doubt the depth of feeling and desire between them, yet he was unaccustomed to it. He sensed his recent acquaintance with his shifter self held the answers to the primitive, visceral need coursing through him. It wasn't simply lust, but lust was certainly the driving force in every interaction with her. From what his mother had told him, he would encounter many shifters in Painter. When he asked her how he would know, she'd told him he would just know. He knew Sophia was a shifter, but damn if he knew how to start a conversation about it. He elected to keep conversation light.

"Well, Quinn's is as busy as you said," he commented.

She smiled and lifted one shoulder in a half-shrug. "It always is. They have good food, good drinks, and good company. Plus, it's pretty affordable. With the ski and college crowd, there are a few high-end places in town. The locals tend to prefer places like Quinn's."

A woman approached their table with a wide grin. She had dark hair and blue eyes. She immediately leaned down to give Sophia a quick hug before turning her disconcertingly direct gaze on him. She arched a brow and held out her hand. "I'm Vivi," she said, her handshake brisk and firm.

"Daniel Hayes," he replied. "Let me guess. You're a friend of Sophia's?"

Vivi released her hand and laughed softly. "Of course. Though you don't have to look far to find one of those in Painter." If he hadn't seen the evidence of that himself tonight, he'd have guessed it. Her nature was warm, friendly and welcoming—yet another quality that drew him to her.

Vivi slid into the booth beside Sophia. "Since I've never seen you around, you must be new to Painter."

Daniel sensed Vivi knew who he was, but she was polite enough to let him tell her. "Depends on what you mean by new. I was born here, but my family moved away when I was only three. I moved here for the summer and maybe longer."

Vivi nodded. "Painter's an awesome town. Do you have any family around?"

Daniel glanced between Sophia and Vivi. "I'm guessing you probably know the answer to that. No need to dance around it. I know what happened to my brother."

Vivi's eyes sobered. "I'm sorry. I didn't mean..."

He cut her off. "It's not like it's easy to bring up my family and how people remember them around here. Painter's not that big. I've had a long damn time to get used to what happened."

Vivi's eyes widened. She nodded firmly. "Okay then. Gotta say, I'm a fan of direct, so I'm glad you just cut through my polite bullshit there."

Her blunt comment made him chuckle, which eased the tension that had sprung up at the table. A waitress arrived to take their orders, and Vivi stood up.

"I'm actually here to work a shift at the bar. Just wanted to say hi since I saw you." She caught Daniel's eyes. "If you like burgers, try Quinn's special. It's got this amazing barbecue sauce. They make it right here." At that, she gave a small wave and turned away, jogging to the bar and ducking behind.

Their waitress was waiting, so they quickly ordered. Daniel decided to follow Vivi's advice and go with the Quinn's special burger. "You a fan of the house burger too?" he asked Sophia.

"Of course! They make a damn good burger here. Nothing too fancy, but delicious."

Dinner passed quickly. There were frequent interruptions from other customers. All the while, Daniel could hardly keep his eyes off of Sophia. His cat simmered under his skin. When their waitress collected their empty plates, Sophia glanced toward the door where there was a cluster of people waiting for tables.

"We should probably go," she said, nodding in the direction of the door.

"Probably." He didn't mind departing per se, but he didn't want the night to end. In fact, he was well past any pretense with himself. He wanted Sophia. *Now.* If he'd learned anything in life, it was that one never knew what might happen. He'd lost a brother he barely remembered, but whose loss echoed in his life to this day. With both of his parents passing away in recent years, the drumbeat of now drove his choices. It's what led him to make plans to move to Painter as soon as he could. The rational, thinking part of his brain told him he shouldn't rush and he should take things slow with Sophia. The feeling part of his brain and body chafed against reason, reminding him again and again he might lose an opportunity if he thought too hard about it. The lion in him merely wanted her with a ferocity unlike anything he'd experienced.

He realized Sophia was waiting. He abruptly made a choice. "We probably should go, but I don't want tonight to end just now."

She held still, a flush moving slowly up her neck and into her cheeks. "Oh. Okay. Um, we can go back to my place if you'd like."

"Sounds good to me." He stood and held his hand out. Sophia placed hers in his, and he pulled her up slowly. When she was standing, he glanced down. Her eyes were dark. He stroked his thumb across her wrist. Her pulse raced under his touch. He felt a slight sense of relief to know she might be as affected as he was.

DAISY GREETED them at the door when they came in. Sophia kicked her shoes off and hung her jacket. "I have to feed her really quick. Just give me a few minutes."

Daisy immediately went to Daniel, nudging his hip with her large head. Daniel followed her toward the kitchen with Daisy shadowing his steps. She'd hoped for a brief respite from the intensity of his presence. Every second with him sent flames licking through her. She hadn't wanted the night to end either, so she'd been simultaneously relieved and anxious when he said as such. Her heart and body were clamoring for him, while her mind kept butting in. *You don't have time for a relationship. You don't even know what he wants. A little fun wouldn't be a bad thing. But what if you want more than a little fun?* Round and round she went in her head.

She quickly got Daisy's food ready and set her bowl on the floor. Daniel had stopped in the archway between the living room and kitchen. His shoulder rested against the wall. His navy gaze held her. She felt caught in a powerful undercurrent. She had no idea how long she stood there frozen in place, but she was knocked out of her trance when Daisy walked past her and curled up on her giant dog bed in the living room. With a satisfied sigh, Daisy promptly fell asleep.

Daniel pushed away from the wall and closed the distance between them in a few strides, stopping right in front of her. His eyes coasted over her face. Her pulse ricocheted wildly. Tendrils of fire slid through her, suffusing her with heat. The air around them compressed, thick with desire.

He cleared his throat, the sound audible in the quiet room. "I'm, uh, not sure what you're going to think, but I think I should say something."

She could barely think over the pounding of her heart and the need clouding her thoughts, but she managed a nod.

"I want you. I'm pretty sure you want me too, so I'd rather not play games if that's okay with you."

His voice was low and gruff. It sent shivers racing through her. Part of her was relieved at his words because they echoed how she felt. Right here, right now in this place where she didn't want to think too hard, she wanted to give herself permission to simply experience whatever lay between them. She couldn't seem to form words, so she took a step toward him. His hands reached for hers, his large palms curling over hers, warm and strong. His touch moved seamlessly, his palms sliding up her arms and past her shoulders. One hand threaded into her hair, cupping the back of her head, while the other slipped around her back, resting in the dip at her waist. She took a shuddering breath and looked up at him.

His head tipped forward. His lips were a fraction away from hers for a second. Her entire being drew taut, anticipation coiling tightly within her center. Suddenly, his mouth crashed against hers. The desire that had been simmering within burst into flames. His hand tightened in her hair, and she savored the pull. His tongue delved deeply, tangling with hers. In seconds, she felt like she was on fire. Their kiss went on and on—hot, wet, deep, and drugging. By the time he tore his mouth free from hers, she was gasping and her pulse was running wild. The scrape of his stubble on her neck notched the heat even higher inside. He traced a path down the column of her neck, along her collarbone and followed the curved edge of her t-shirt.

She stroked her hands under his shirt, gasping at the feel of his hard muscles under her palms. His hand slipped loose from her hair, sliding down her back in a heated stroke before dipping under the edge of her t-shirt and sliding back up. With a flick of his thumb, her bra came undone and his palms came around to curl over her breasts. His touch was sheer relief—her breasts were hot, heavy, and aching for his touch. He took his time, his thumbs stroking back and forth over her nipples, teasing her to near madness. She could feel the heat of his shaft in the cradle of her hips and arched against it, seeking relief from the liquid need building and building between her thighs.

His hands stilled, and he pulled back a fraction. Wildness spun within, pushing against her. His eyes held hers, dark and intent. "We need to stop now if we're stopping." He bit the words out with his jaw clenched tightly.

She couldn't have stopped if she wanted, so powerful was the need rushing through her. She was driven only by the need to have him—completely. She didn't know if it was because it had been so damn long since she'd been with anyone, or if it was because the attraction to Daniel was its own primal, pulsing force. She didn't care to ponder it just now. She realized he was waiting for her reply as they stood there. The air around them nearly vibrated with the tension. "I don't want to stop." Her words came out raspy, rough from the edges of her desire.

He nodded sharply and took a step back. Cool air filled the space between them. She felt bereft and experienced a moment of confusion until he spoke. "Bedroom?" His palm curled around one of her hands, warm and strong.

"Oh, right. Over there." She gestured to the small alcove on the far side of the living room.

He turned, her hand held firmly in his, and led the way through the door into her bedroom. Her bed had been passed on to her from her grandmother. It was a large four-poster bed with a canopy above. She'd wound gauzy white fabric through the canopy, so the light fell through in muted shades. Pillows were piled high in many colors. Daniel sat on the foot of the bed and tugged her into the space between his knees. His hands rested on her hips. His eyes held hers as he slowly slid his hands up, catching the edge of her t-shirt and dragging it up. The fabric bunched under his hands as they coasted up her sides. By the time her shirt was lifted up and over her head, she was nearly dizzy with need. Her breath came in shallow gasps. Her t-shirt fell to the floor in a slow arc as he tossed it loose. She shook out of her bra. She experienced a flash of self-consciousness, which dissolved the instant she caught his eyes on her. They were dark with desire.

He proceeded to drive her mad with his hands and mouth. He started just above the waist of her jeans—kisses, soft and rough, the scrape of his stubble on her skin, the calloused surface of his palms tracing circles. He mapped his way up her abdomen slowly, so slowly, she thought she might die of need by the time his lips coasted along the undersides of her breasts. Her nipples were peaked tight. He caught them between his thumb and forefinger, lightly pinching before his lips finally closed over one. A low moan tore from her throat at the relief. He alternated between them until she was arching and flexing against him, frantic to be closer.

She yanked at his t-shirt. He reached behind his head and lifted it up and off in one smooth motion. She got only a glimpse of the glory of his muscled chest—all hard planes—before he pulled her against him. She sighed at the feel of him against her. He was so tall that seated on her bed, they were nearly level. He caught her lips in a kiss—slow, wet, and deep—while his hands stroked up her back, bringing her flush against him.

She needed more, and she needed it now. She took a step back, ran her hands down his chest and tore his jeans open. She curled her palm around his cock, hot and hard under his briefs. His breath hissed through his teeth, and he moved swiftly. He stood and turned, lifting her up and stretching her out on the bed. In seconds, he'd tugged her jeans down. She kicked them loose and watched while he peeled his off. He stood at the foot of the bed in a pair of black briefs, his arousal more than evident. He leaned over and lifted his jeans. He tugged his wallet out and out of that a condom, which he tossed to her nightstand, his aim dead on.

With the burn of his gaze on her, Daniel stretched out beside her. The air shimmered around them, heavy with need and longing. Sophia was nearly overcome with the depth of sheer want rolling through her. She waited, barely able to breathe, as his eyes traveled up her body. He lifted a hand and dragged the backs of his fingers slowly up her abdomen, tracing lazy circles around her nipples. Every touch was like sparks on tinder, fanning the flames higher and higher. He traced up and then back down over the curve of her belly. Her sex clenched, drenched with need. He cupped his palm over her mound, that subtle pressure nearly causing her to orgasm right then and there. She shifted her legs restlessly and gasped his name.

He dragged a finger over the black silk between her thighs. Back and forth, back and forth, grazing the nub of her desire. Her hips arched into his touch. Suddenly frantic, she rolled over and straddled him. His cock rested between her thighs. The slow burn flashed hot and high. The next few moments were a blur as she curled her legs and rolled her hips against him—streaks of pleasure arcing through her with every nudge of his cock against her. He rolled them over again and stretched her arms above her head, her wrists held firm in his grip. With his other hand, he yanked her underwear off and kicked his own loose. For a long moment, he froze above her and then dipped his head, catching her lips in a fierce kiss. She heard the tear of foil and then felt the tip of his cock at her entrance.

DANIEL FORCED himself to hold still. His pulse pounded while need clawed at him. Sophia's eyes met his, her green gaze hazy and dark. She curled her legs around his hips and arched into him. In a swift surge, he sank into the creamy clench of her channel. Her gasp fed the fire raging through him. He wanted to go slow, to savor this, but he couldn't. His need was too primal and ran too deep. He managed several long, slow strokes, biting back a groan at the feel of her slick channel throbbing around him. When his name fell from her lips in a gasp, the reins on his control broke. He pounded into her with deep surges. Tremors ran through her, and her head thrashed wildly against the pillows. A heady satisfaction coursed through him when she cried out and arched into him, her nails scoring his back. He let loose with a growl, his body going rigid just before his release came. He fell against her, immediately shifting his weight to the side so as not to crush her. Their mingled gasps were the only sound in the room.

7

Sophia slowly drifted down from the heady sensations coursing through her. Daniel had untangled himself a few moments ago and stepped into the bathroom to dispose of his condom. He'd immediately returned to the bed and tugged her close. Her body was only now beginning to cool. His palm was warm on her back, moving in slow circles. As the pounding beat of desire quieted now that her need had been slaked, awareness sifted into her consciousness. She had enough sense to know what had just transpired between them was far beyond what she'd expected. She wasn't quite ready to face what that might mean for her, so she shook the thoughts away.

When she woke, the first rays of sun were angling across her bed. Daniel was sound asleep beside her, his hand resting on her hip. What she wanted was to stay here all day and explore more of him. Yet, she had to go to work and needed time to sort through the muddle of confusion between her mind, body and heart. She carefully untangled her legs and sat up. When she glanced back at Daniel, his eyes were open and alert.

"Morning," he offered with a half-smile.

She flushed instantly, and then flushed even deeper. "Good morning. I have to get to the coffee shop."

"I figured," he said softly. He drew his hand slowly over the curve up her hip, into the dip of her waist and up over the curve of her breast. His touch sent sparks through her while warmth curled around her heart. She loved the easy feeling with him. When she glanced over at him, he rolled his head to the side and caught her lips in a quick kiss before he moved swiftly and threw the covers back. As he stood, she couldn't keep her eyes off of his body. He was simply a work of art, honed muscle from head to toe with that lean, coiled energy shifters carried. He paused by the bathroom door. "Coming?"

Her confusion must have shown because he clarified. "Shower?"

"Oh, right." She stood and hurried after him. He was all business in the shower until the end. Just as she was about to step out, he slipped a hand around her waist and tugged her close for a kiss. In seconds, she was nearly on fire again. He pulled back, a wry grin curling the corners of his mouth. "Didn't mean to go too far," he said with a soft chuckle. He shook his head sharply. "You have to go to work, and so do I."

They dressed quickly. Daisy was waiting patiently by the door. She nudged Daniel's hip and followed them into the kitchen. After Sophia fed Daisy and let her run around outside, she grabbed an apple from the bowl of fruit she kept on the counter and held one up for Daniel. At his nod, she tossed it to him.

"You want me to drop you off at work?" he asked.

She hesitated, but usually she'd walk, so there was no reason not to accept a ride. "Sure. I'll walk home later."

When he pulled up in front of Mile High Grounds, she turned toward him. Before she had a chance to think, he leaned across the console and brushed his lips across hers. That brief point of contact sent heat swirling through her center. Her belly fluttered, and her breath caught. When she looked up, his eyes reflected the desire she felt.

SOPHIA WAS WALKING around her house watering plants when there was a knock at the door. As she turned toward it, the door opened and Heath walked through. She set the watering can down on a side table, ran to her brother and threw her arms around him. "I'm so glad you're home!"

Heath hugged her tightly before stepping back. His green eyes, so similar to hers, were warm and steady. The old clarity and confidence he used to convey had returned. He'd lost it for a while after his accident. There was an added layer of humility in his gaze. It had hurt to watch, but her brother had been brought low in the domino chain of events following his car accident. She squeezed his hands before releasing them.

"How are you?" she asked.

Heath nodded firmly. "Believe it or not, pretty damn good. I hated to end up there, but rehab was the best choice for me. Honestly, the arrest scared me straight, but I needed the time to recoup. I can think clearly again. Plus, they had a sweet gym on site, so I put myself through the paces and finally feel physically healthy again." He ran a hand through his dark hair and took a breath. "How are things with you?"

She shrugged. "The usual. Busy at Mile High."

Heath nodded. "Mom and Dad stopped by this morning. Things seem...better with them," he said, his voice hitching at the end.

She knew he'd been struggling with guilt over how hard his accident and everything afterwards had hit their parents. "Mom and Dad are fine. I know I'm probably wasting my breath, but try to not feel so shitty about the whole thing. You're safe and healthy and that's all that matters." Heath nodded tightly and reached down to stroke Daisy who'd come to sit by his feet. "Come on in. Believe it or not, I need some coffee. I got so busy at work this afternoon, I never bothered to have any," Sophia said, gesturing for him to follow her.

She walked into the kitchen and quickly started a fresh pot of coffee. Heath sat down at the kitchen table with Daisy shadowing him and sitting by his side. Daisy adored Heath. Sophia sat across from him. "Are you hungry?"

He shook his head. "Nah. I'm good."

There was a long silence before Heath cleared his throat. "I hate asking, but any word on the police investigation into the smuggling network?"

She leaned back in her chair and sighed. "I wish there was, but no. If there's any news, I haven't heard. I'm guessing they're trying to keep things quiet even if they have leads." She considered whether to talk to him about her and Vivi's efforts. After a moment of indecision, she decided honesty was necessary. After all he'd been through, she didn't want to hide anything.

"Vivi and I have been doing a little scouting of our own."

Heath's eyes widened and his mouth tightened at the corners. "Soph, what the hell are you thinking?"

"You'd do the same thing if you watched me go through what you have!" Her simmering anger flashed any time she was reminded of what Heath had been through.

He was still for several beats before he sighed, the sound weary and worn. "I know, I know. I just don't want you to get caught in the crosshairs. Those guys aren't messing around. They're making money and won't let anyone get in the way of that. How about you back off and let the police do their jobs?"

"Because they're not doing a damn thing! You get arrested for trying to buy drugs while they can't seem to arrest any dealers other than the two-bit guys you were trying to buy from. In the meantime, nobody trusts anyone anymore. The whole thing makes me sick. Honestly, I tried to ignore it for the last few years. I kept thinking it would just go away and then everything went to shit for you. Now I'm just pissed about it."

Heath shook his head slowly. "Don't go blaming the shifters smuggling for me getting hooked on painkillers. That's my cross to bear."

Sophia looked over at Heath. Her heart clenched at the weary resignation on his face. She picked up a pen on the table and twirled it between her fingers. "It's not that. I'm just sick of the situation. I know you're responsible for you, but it doesn't change the fact that the shifters involved in this are putting all of us at risk. Have you been following the news? They've managed to shut it down in Catamount back in Maine. All we need is enough shifters to care, so we can put a stop to it. Well, that and figuring out who the hell started the whole dame thing. Anyway, Vivi and I haven't gotten anywhere really, but we did find a remote location we think they might be using."

His eyes narrowed. "Really?"

She nodded. "Yup. Vivi hears talk all the time when she covers shifts at Quinn's. She heard a few rumors, so we decided to take a look. It's an old abandoned cabin on the far side of town, pretty deep in the woods."

"Wonder if I've ever seen it," Heath questioned aloud.

She shrugged. "Maybe. If you did, it was when you were out wandering. If we hadn't shifted, it would have taken hours to hike out there. There were two men there when we first saw the cabin. We think Randy and Doyle showed up to meet with the guys there."

His brows hitched up. "Really? Hmm. If it was Randy and Doyle, it's definitely a place to watch. It's not like I knew them well, but they were pretty into the drug scene. Did you get a good look at the other guys?"

"Nope. They had their backs to us the whole time."

Heath was quiet for another moment before he shook his head sharply. "Enough of this. I'm not gonna stuff my head in the sand, but I don't want my first day back to be all about this fucking mess. Tell me what else is going on with you."

Sophia was happy to drop the topic and moved onto much lighter matters. Somewhere along the way, she mentioned Daniel, thinking Heath would hear about him soon enough. She was already hearing rumbles from the rumor mill about his appearance in town. The unfortunate memory associated with his brother had faded, yet it held its place in Painter's shifter history. She was so relieved Daniel had already known what happened to his brother before he came to Painter in search of his family's history.

"Wait, the kid who got shot when he shifted? It's his brother who moved to town?" Heath asked.

"That's the one. Daniel Hayes. I met him when he stopped by Mile High for coffee." She elected not to elaborate further on just how thoroughly she'd become acquainted with Daniel. Simply saying his name aloud sent heat flooding through her. She was mightily relieved to have the coffee maker beep its readiness, giving her an excuse to stand and busy herself filling mugs of coffee and bringing creamer to the table.

At that moment, Daisy rose from where she'd been napping on the floor under the kitchen table and woofed softly. As Sophia turned to glance toward the front door, Vivi's head poked around the door.

"Hey there," Vivi called with a wave.

"Hey, come on in! Heath's here."

Daisy met Vivi as she passed through the archway into the kitchen. Vivi stroked Daisy quickly and threw her arms around Heath when he stood to greet her.

"You're home!"

Heath chuckled as he stepped away and sat down again. "It's damn good to be here."

"Want some coffee?" Sophia asked Vivi.

Vivi nodded and joined Heath at the table. "I could use the extra kick. Julianna was up half the night after my mom let her take a three hour nap yesterday afternoon." Vivi groaned. "I love that my mom helps with babysitting, but she has completely blanked out how important it is not to let kids nap too long. I woke up at two in the morning when I heard Julianna having tea with one of her dolls." Vivi rolled her eyes before taking a healthy gulp of the coffee Sophia handed over.

A while later, Heath waved from the door before he closed it behind him. Sophia's heart was warm and full. For the first time in over a year, she had a nice afternoon with her brother and a friend. Nothing other than coffee and lazy chatting. Heath was headed over to their parents' home to help their father move some old furniture out of the barn.

She glanced at Vivi whose eyes were wistful.

"What's got that look on your face?" she asked.

Vivi smiled softly and shrugged. "Just nice to see Heath finally looking like himself again."

Sophia nodded slowly. "I know. It's pretty damn awesome."

Vivi grinned and wrinkled her nose. She held her coffee mug out. "Any coffee left?"

Sophia swiped it from her hand and leaned back,

quickly refilling Vivi's mug without bothering to get up. "There you go." She slid it across the table.

Vivi's eyes took on a gleam. "So? Planning to fill me in on your date with Daniel? It's been radio silence all day, and it's killing me. I'll cut you a little slack since Heath just got back, but now you'd better give it up."

Sophia's cheeks felt hot. She'd known it was only a matter of time before Vivi brought Daniel up, but Sophia was no more clear in her thoughts about him than she had been last night when they were skin to skin. In every free moment today, he'd strolled through her thoughts. There was the way she felt when she was skin to skin with him, which was like nothing she'd ever experienced. Then, there was her rational brain, or more accurately her human brain, chiming in on how she needed to not let her body run away with this and convince her he was more than he was.

"Oh God, Viv, I don't know." She ran her hands through her hair with a sigh.

"Well, you had dinner with him. I know that. It can't have been dinner that's got you so worked up. I mean, he's hot, but..."

"Oh, it was more than dinner. A lot more."

Vivi squealed. "Well, hot damn. You finally broke your self-imposed no-sex rule. Great news as far as I'm concerned!" She paused for a sip of coffee, her eyes sobering. "Okay, what's got you so freaked out?"

Sophia felt so emotional, tears pressed against her eyelids. She shrugged. "I don't know. I'm all a mess inside. I didn't have a no-sex rule by the way. Why do you insist on saying that?" she asked with a roll of her eyes.

Vivi mimicked her eye-roll with a chuckle. "Because you haven't dated anyone in forever. That's why."

"Well, neither have you," Sophia countered.

Vivi shrugged. "I have a better excuse. I'm a single mom

who learned the hard way love isn't all it's cracked up to be." She was referring to Julianna's father who'd made himself scarce for most of Julianna's life. The blush had most definitely faded on that rose once responsibility came calling.

Sophia sighed and shook her head. "Maybe you think it's a good excuse, but still." At Vivi's sigh, she returned back to Vivi's question about Daniel. "Maybe I'm all a mess because this thing with Daniel...it's intense. It's more than I bargained for and now I'm worried I'm in over my head. I mean, now is not the time for me to start a relationship. I've got too much going on with work, I need to be there for Heath and my parents, I don't even know what Daniel wants or how long he's going to be here, and..."

Vivi made the time out sign with her hands and cut in. "Okay, okay. Slow the hell down and breathe."

Sophia put her face in her hands and forced herself to take several slow breaths. When she looked up, Vivi's warm eyes were on her. "Sorry, that turned into a babble. Long story short, I just don't know."

Vivi nodded slowly. "Clearly. But you also like him. A lot."

Sophia's face felt like it was on fire. "Well, I don't know..." Her words trailed off when Vivi arched a brow.

"You don't need to pretend with me. I saw the way you look at him. I mean, I'll be the first to say, the man is seriously easy on the eyes, but I can manage to look at him and just appreciate a good thing. You're practically buzzing when you're near him."

Sophia didn't know how it was possible, but she blushed even harder. "That obvious, huh?" It unnerved her to realize how blatant her attraction to him was.

Vivi nodded wryly. "Hey, it's not exactly bad to be into someone who's clearly just as into you."

Her belly somersaulted and hope tap-danced in her heart. "You think?"

Vivi grinned. "Uh, yeah. You two were in your own little world. I'm amazed you didn't melt each other on sight."

Sophia giggled and then sobered. "That's good to know, but it doesn't change the fact I don't exactly have time…"

Vivi threw her hands up in time out again. "Stop it! Stop throwing up all these barriers. You will always be busy with work. That's life. Sure, it's been an eventful and difficult year for your family. You know damn well the last thing they want is you putting your life on hold all because you think you have to give every second of your spare time to them. You can be there for Heath and your parents and have a life. Honestly, it's probably better for Heath if you're not hovering. He's got to do this on his own."

Sophia took a deep breath and idly traced the edge of the fruit bowl on the table. "I know," she said softly. "I don't mean to make it seem like I'm putting up barriers. I just wasn't expecting to like Daniel this much. There's also the tiny issue that I don't even know how much he knows about shifters and how long he'll be in Painter."

Vivi sighed dramatically. "Okay. Right, that could be an issue. He's definitely a shifter. Everyone in his mother's family was a shifter, not to mention he oozes the whole shifter vibe. Regardless of what he knows or doesn't know, the reality is he'll have to come to terms with it one way or another. Maybe you should just ask him about it."

At Sophia's wide eyes, Vivi chuckled and stood up, carrying her coffee mug to the sink. She leaned her hips against the counter when she turned back. "You know me, I'm all about just getting it over with."

She stepped to Sophia's side and dropped a kiss on her cheek. "Gotta go. Julianna's bus will be here any minute." At that, she stroked Daisy quickly and raced out the door.

8

Daniel drove down the winding lane that led to his uncle's home, his mother's childhood home. The old farmhouse was set back from the road, nestled at the base of the mountains. It was a two-story home with a wrap-around porch and simple white siding. Its age was showing with the paint peeling in areas. The yard was overgrown. A lone car was parked in front of the house. He came to a stop and turned the engine off. Quiet settled around him. He didn't want to be, but he was nervous. He'd tried calling his uncle with no luck. The man didn't appear to have a listed number and had essentially no online footprint. His knowledge of his mother's family had been a void until she finally shared the truth before she died. He'd had a year to absorb the fact he was a shifter, come to terms with the truth behind how his brother died, and now he was about to meet the last living member of his mother's family.

He stepped out swiftly and paused to glance around. What looked to be a many years overgrown garden was off to one side of the house. A stand of aspen was on the other side. The house faced toward downtown Painter. The picturesque town peeked out of the trees. The mountains rose steeply behind the home, marching skyward. He took a breath and jogged up the stairs. After knocking on the door, he waited long enough he began to wonder if anyone was home. Just as he was about to try knocking once more, the door opened.

A man stood there. He was tall, just a shade shorter than Daniel who was taller than average at six foot three inches. He had mostly gray hair and faded blue eyes. Daniel couldn't have said what he expected, but it wasn't this. The man's expression was flat. He arched a brow. "Can I help you?"

"I was looking for Nelson Weaver. You wouldn't happen to be him, would you?"

A small part of Daniel hoped this man wasn't because he was anything but welcoming. The man cocked his head to the side and nodded slowly.

"I'm Nelson. Who are you?"

"I'm Daniel Hayes, your nephew." The words were difficult to force out.

Nelson's eyes widened. "Holy shit," he muttered. "What the hell are you doing in Painter?"

Daniel considered his words for a moment and decided to be just as blunt as Nelson. "My mother died last year. She finally told me what happened to David and why we moved away. Before I knew all that, she talked a lot about Painter and how much she missed it. I decided to come see the place she loved so much and see if I could reconnect with any family. As far as I can find out, you're the only family left in the area."

Nelson stepped back from the door and gestured for Daniel to come in. He still didn't seem warm and friendly, although he was clearly curious. Daniel followed him inside and looked around. They passed through a foyer.

Directly ahead was a staircase. There were archways on either side of the foyer. One led into a kitchen and the other into a living room area. The home held an empty quality, almost as if no one really lived here. The living room furniture was covered in sheets and didn't appear to be in use. Nelson led the way into the kitchen. It was a large, country style kitchen with an antique porcelain stove in the center of the far wall with counters circling the room. A large island separated the kitchen from a dining area, which was a table built into a nook with windows on all three sides. More of the overgrown yard was visible.

While this area didn't appear to be entirely out of use, Nelson clearly spent little time here. A single plate sat in a drying rack by the sink. Nelson sat down at the table and gestured for Daniel to join him. Daniel slid into the bench seat across from Nelson, wondering what to say next. Nelson finally spoke again.

"This is where your mother and I grew up. She loved this old house."

For a flicker, Daniel saw pain in Nelson's eyes, but it was shuttered quickly. It occurred to him that Nelson had been the one to be here to watch his parents grow old in the aftermath of David's tragic death. Daniel's mother had shared she had only occasional visits with her parents in the years after they moved away and that she lost touch with her brother entirely after their parents passed away.

Daniel nodded. "She mentioned the house. She wasn't even sure it was still in the family."

Nelson shrugged. "Yeah, we didn't really stay in touch. Things were rough after your brother died."

"That's what my mom said." Daniel felt off kilter and uncertain what was okay to ask about. His brother's death was like a bell that wouldn't stop ringing in his life. He was too young to remember much about David. He'd only been three when David died. He carried a vague memory of a brother who let him sit by him and watch cartoons. More vividly, he recalled the heavy silence that shrouded David's memory for most of his childhood. What he knew now put it into perspective. His mother carried immense guilt over her little boy shifting unexpectedly in a park. His father carried anger mixed with guilt. Daniel had never had a chance to ask his father about David's death with the truth helping to guide his questions. What he remembered about his parents' marriage was they had been deeply in love, a love not often seen. Daniel could look back now and recognize his father's anger over David's death and the guilt of feeling that anger. In retrospect, he wouldn't have been surprised if something such as David's death could have torn a family apart. Memories of his parents tumbled through his thoughts as he looked across at Nelson. Somehow, the word "rough" didn't seem to do justice to what David's death had meant to his family.

Daniel took a breath. "If you're wondering, I know how David died." He thought it better to make sure that was clear.

Nelson eyed him for a long moment and nodded sharply. "Alright then. How, uh, how did Sarah die?"

Daniel's heart squeezed, a lingering pang of grief. "Pneumonia. It got bad fast. She never turned it around. She was at peace by the time she died."

Nelson was quiet. "I'm sorry I wasn't there."

Daniel shrugged. "Like you said, you lost touch. From what I knew, my parents steered clear of Painter and anyone connected to it after they moved away."

"That they did."

Another long silence. Daniel cleared his throat. "Look, I wanted a chance to meet anyone left from my family."

"I'm it, at least around Painter. We have some cousins scattered around Colorado, but I haven't stayed in touch with anyone. If you know how David died, then you know that event blew a hole through the shifter community. My parents never really got over it. They pretty much holed themselves up here until they died. I mind my own business. Memories are long in the shifter world. No one forgets. No one blamed David, but what happened put us all at risk. It's been a long damn time."

Daniel had been prepared for this because his mother had warned him. "I know. We don't have to dwell on the heavy stuff. Maybe you can tell me what you do, show me around the house, that kind of thing?"

Nelson was quiet for a beat. The man wasn't much for conversation that was for sure. "Not much to say. I work for myself doing odd jobs. You're welcome to take a look around the house. I only use a few parts of it. In case you were wondering, it's deeded to you when I pass away. My parents set it up that way before they died."

Uncertain how to respond, Daniel nodded. Over the next half hour, Nelson took Daniel on a cursory tour of the house. As Daniel drove away, the farmhouse fading to a speck in his rear view mirror, he considered that he'd met his uncle and wasn't inclined to see him again. Nelson left him feeling unsettled. His uncle was distant and guarded to an unusual degree. The only moment when he'd sensed any possibility of warmth was when Nelson had mentioned how Daniel's mother had loved the house. Daniel couldn't put his finger on it, but he sensed Nelson's life had turned onto an unsavory path in the years since David's death. He was glad for having met him, but he sensed their meeting would be no more than it was.

He found himself driving straight toward downtown Painter and heading to Mile High Grounds. He wanted to see Sophia. No, he *needed* to see Sophia.

Sophia quickly prepped another espresso and passed it to Josie. They were in a rhythm. It had been a busy afternoon. She was functioning on autopilot. Tommy caught her eye and mouthed to her. "Bathroom break." She nodded to him.

"Josie, I'm taking the counter while Tommy grabs a break. Why don't you take one after he gets back?"

Josie nodded. "Sure."

As Sophia stepped to the counter, Josie immediately picked up the pace, making two coffees at a time. Sophia entered into the fray of customers, bantering with the regulars. Tommy returned and took over for Josie. The customers eventually began to thin out as they entered into late afternoon. Sophia loved this time of day at the coffee shop. The afternoon sun fell in a slant through the windows, bathing the coffee shop in a soft glow. Customers who were here this time of day tended to be quiet. She usually had time to get caught up in the afternoon. Josie started tidying the shelves of coffee mugs and other supplies they sold out front, while Tommy hunkered down in the back kitchen and prepped pastries for the next day.

Sophia remained at the counter and switched the computer screen over to her supply-ordering page. She worked hard to purchase locally sourced, organic coffee beans and to order organic baking supplies as well. She had a few preferred suppliers and got to work on this month's order. She was so focused she didn't hear the next customer approach the counter.

"Sophia?"

Daniel's voice, low and gravelly, hit her right in her center. Tendrils of heat swirled outward through her body. Her eyes whipped up, slamming into his navy gaze. The air instantly came to life around them, as if lit by a flame. They were both still for a long, taut moment. Sophia finally shook her head. The corner of Daniel's mouth curled in a half-smile.

"You seem to do that a lot."

She bit her lip to keep from laughing.

"What is it with you making me shake my head?"

"Don't go blaming me for that."

"Okay, you're not making me shake my head. It just seems like I can't think straight when you're around." She flushed suddenly, aware her words were far more accurate than she might have intended.

"Well, that makes two of us then."

Daniel's gaze darkened. Sophia's pulse skittered, and her breath hitched. Another customer approached at that moment. Daniel stepped to the side. "Go ahead," he gestured to the woman.

"What can I get for you?" Sophia asked brightly, trying to quell her racing heart. To say Daniel was distracting was a massive understatement. Her body was like a live wire when he was near.

The young woman brushed her blonde hair behind her ears and fiddled with a silver hoop bracelet while she read the chalkboard menu behind the counter. "I'll take a mocha latte."

Sophia turned to call out to Tommy who quickly paused in what he was doing and caught her eyes. "Already on it," he said with a grin. He stepped forward from the baking area in the back and immediately began prepping the latte. Sophia rang the woman up and handed over her change.

Daniel was leaning against the wall by the counter, a hand in his jeans pocket. The planes of his muscled chest filled out his navy t-shirt. Her mind flashed to the feel of his chest under her hands and against her body. Another wash of heat rolled through her. Tommy stepped to her side, sliding the woman's latte across the counter. "There you go," Tommy said. After the woman walked away, Tommy turned, his eyes catching hers from the side. "Planning to introduce me to your friend?" he asked just above a whisper.

She flushed straight through. "Of course." She glanced to Daniel as Tommy turned back to the counter. "Daniel, this is Tommy Dawson."

Daniel stepped to the counter and reached across to shake Tommy's hand. "Daniel Hayes. Nice to meet you."

Tommy grinned, his brown eyes twinkling. "Nice to meet you. How long have you been in Painter?"

"Just moved here recently. I've already found my favorite coffee shop," he replied with a grin.

Tommy chuckled. "Mile High's the best in town."

A couple stepped to the counter. Sophia waited on them while Daniel and Tommy continued chatting. Josie made her way back behind the counter. The next hour or so rolled by. Daniel ended up in the small kitchen area in back keeping Tommy company and assisting with the pastry prep for the following morning. He and Tommy had gotten onto the topic of computer coding. Sophia experienced an odd mix of feelings about Daniel's easy comfort. Part of her thrilled to it, while another part of her kept warning against letting herself get too comfortable. Either way, he spent the afternoon there, leaving her flushed and flustered every time her eyes landed on him. When it came time to close, Tommy and Josie waved her off, insisting they'd close up. She was reluctant at first, but she couldn't resist the pull to have Daniel to herself. Daniel followed her outside.

She paused on the sidewalk. The sun was setting behind the mountains. The sky was swirled in gold, orange and red. The decorative streetlights blinked on. She turned to face Daniel. He stood quietly, his hands in his pockets. He'd been looking up toward the sunset, but his eyes swung down to meet hers the moment she turned. "I was hoping I could see you tonight."

The only answer was yes. She nodded wordlessly. Emotion tightened her chest. This intensity of emotion Daniel elicited in her was startling. He took two strides to stand in front of her. He didn't say a word. His eyes held hers—banked heat and understanding reflected in them. He dipped his head and caught her lips in a kiss. It was just a kiss, a quick brush of his lips across hers before he caught her lower lip in his teeth, tugging softly as he pulled away. Heat flooded her body, liquid need swirling in her center.

He remained close. Her hand had landed on his chest, and she could feel his heart pounding. A small sense of relief washed through her to know he was perhaps as affected by her as she was by him. He cleared his throat. "Did you walk into town today?"

She nodded, trying to catch her breath and slow the wild flutter of her pulse. "Should we grab dinner in town?"

She shook her head firmly. She might be diving headfirst into madness, but she needed him to herself now. "Let's have dinner at my place again. Daisy will be expecting me home soon anyway."

Daniel smiled slowly. "Dinner at your place sounds perfect."

9

———

Daniel stood in Sophia's kitchen, chopping onions rapidly. Daisy was lounging in the middle of the kitchen, taking up most of the floor with her sprawling frame. After they'd gotten to Sophia's house, she'd fed Daisy and declared she would cook a stir-fry. Daniel offered to help and next thing he knew, she'd assigned him to chopping the vegetables while she busied herself slicing chicken. He took a swallow of wine from the glass she'd set beside the cutting board for him.

When he was with her, he felt a sense of comfort and easiness. Just now, he felt as if they'd done this hundreds of times before. All they were doing was cooking dinner together. The only unsettling thing was Daniel didn't know what to do with the depth of his feelings. Not to mention the nearly overwhelming attraction that sizzled to life between them whenever they were within sight of each other.

When they sat down to eat, he finally asked the question he'd been wanting to ask since he'd visited his uncle. "Are you a shifter?"

Sophia was in the middle of lifting her fork to her mouth. Her hand froze in mid-air, and her eyes widened. She slowly set her fork down. She looked at him, her gaze searching. After several beats of silence, she nodded slowly. "I am. Everyone in my family is a shifter. I'm guessing you have your reasons for asking."

Daniel considered his reply. He bought himself a little time by taking a bite of food. "I only found out shifters existed outside of rumors right before my mother died. She gave me a crash course in our family history in just a few weeks and explained why I could hardly tolerate going hiking in the woods anymore."

Sophia had resumed eating. She paused between bites and took a healthy gulp of wine. "Wow. That must have been... I don't know, really. How are you with all of it?"

Daniel took a swallow of wine and considered her question. He was aware he could have been shocked, terrified, confused and many other possible feelings, yet once he'd heard everything from his mother, he felt mostly relieved. Deep down, he'd known he was somehow different. The questions tumbling about inside had been answered once his mother shared the truth of who and what he was. He looked over at Sophia who was patiently waiting for his answer. "I won't say it wasn't startling at first, but it all made sense. I'm okay with all of it. I'm sorry for how my brother died and for what that did to my family, but I'm relieved to know the whole truth." He paused, considering whether to talk with her about his uncle. He decided he might as well. "I went by to meet my uncle today."

Her eyes widened slightly. "How'd that go?"

"Not great really. He's not the friendliest guy. I meant to ask if maybe you could introduce me to your mom like you said, so I could ask her about my family. Nelson was pretty quiet. What do you know about him?"

She shook her head slowly. "Not much really. I haven't

seen him around in years. My mother would be able to offer more. All I know is he stays out at your family's old property and keeps to himself. I'll call my mom tomorrow and bring you out to meet her." She paused for a sip of wine. "Not to get too nosy, but how does it feel to know you're a shifter?"

"On some level, I knew something was up whenever I was hiking in the woods and thought my body was going to explode. When my mom finally told me everything, it was kind of a relief once I got used to the idea."

"I'm trying to imagine what it would be like to learn something that big that far into life. I've known I was a shifter for as long as I can remember. Painter has a pretty large shifter community, so it's impossible to be one around here and not know and hear about others. It seems like it would have been lonely to learn the way you did."

"I suppose it was, but there's not much I can do about it now. That's a big part of why I came to Painter. My mom told me I'd be able to meet other shifters here. I know they're probably everywhere, but I wanted to come to the place where my family came from."

Sophia nodded. "Shifters are everywhere, but Painter and a few other communities are strongholds. My family moved here a few generations back from Catamount, Maine, which is where shifters were first born. I'm allegedly a descendant of a founding shifter family."

Daniel couldn't help the curl of curiosity. He wanted to know so much, it was difficult to corral his questions. Sophia didn't seem to mind and happily answered anything he asked about the shifter community. Dinner passed quickly. Before he knew it, Sophia was clearing plates from the table and loading them in the dishwasher. He stood up from the table and carried their empty wineglasses to hand to her. Her fingers brushed his, and a jolt of lust rocked him. The current between them never died out. It ebbed and flowed, but it was always present.

Her dark hair swung over her shoulder as she leaned down and placed the two glasses in the dishwasher before she closed it. She wore a pair of black leggings and a fitted emerald green t-shirt. She'd kicked off her cowboy boots by the door. She turned to face him, her hands curling on the edge of the counter. His heart pounded, strong and steady. The simmer of lust within threatened to boil over. He itched to grab her, toss her over his shoulder and carry her straight to the bedroom. Daisy, who happened to occupy most of the floor, stretched and sighed.

Daniel met Sophia's eyes, that gorgeous green gaze, and saw desire darken them. He stepped around Daisy and reached for Sophia's hand. The moment his palm closed around hers, the pounding beat of lust intensified. He didn't care to bother to take things slowly just now. Though not a word passed between them, her dark gaze and the rapid flutter of the pulse in her wrist told him what he needed to know. He turned and stepped past Daisy, Sophia's hand firmly in his. When he reached her bedroom door, he glanced over his shoulder. She reached past him and gave the door a soft push. He stepped through with her right behind him. He didn't wait and turned to face her, fitting his mouth over hers.

The embers inside flashed into white-hot flames as she arched into him and gasped against his mouth. He swept his tongue inside, emitting a low growl when her tongue met his stroke for stroke. He flattened a palm against the door behind her as he tore his lips from hers, licking and nipping his way down her neck. He could barely keep himself in check when he curled a palm around her breast and felt the tight bead of her nipple through the thin cotton of her t-shirt.

His lion simmered under his skin, rumbling for more.

Now. He needed to taste her, to know every inch of her. The next few moments passed in a frantic blur. He tore at her clothes, ripping her t-shirt down the center and shoving her leggings down. She was as frantic as he was, shoving his t-shirt up and tossing it across the room. She swiftly unbuttoned his jeans and started to slide her palm around his cock, but he couldn't be distracted just yet.

He hooked a hand under her knee and stroked a finger into her cleft. Her head slammed against the door behind her as her breath came out in a long hiss. She was drenched, so wet all he could think about was how good it would feel to be inside of her. Somehow, he grabbed onto a thin thread of control. He might be teetering on the edge of madness, but he meant to make her forget everything but him, to imprint himself on her as deeply as she'd already imprinted herself on him. The beat of lust pounded through him as he slowly dragged his fingers back and forth through her folds. When he eased one finger and then another into her channel, she clenched around him.

He knelt down, glancing up for a moment as he did. Her dark hair fell in a tangle around her shoulders. Her dusky nipples peeked out through the curtain of her hair. Her full breasts were enough to bring him to his knees, so it was good he was already there. Her breath came in pants and gasps. Her eyes flickered open, her gaze hazy with passion. Holding her eyes until the last moment, he leaned forward and brought his mouth to her center. Her hips bucked against him. He gripped her hips with one hand, savoring the give of her flesh under his grip, and set out to taste and pleasure every inch of her. Her breath came in broken gasps and low moans. He licked and stroked, establishing a steady rhythm with his fingers. Her thighs were wet from her own desire and her head thrashed against the door. Her channel began to throb around his fingers. Only then did he swirl his tongue around her the nub of her desire once more. Her cries rained down over him as he dragged his fingers out and slowly rose.

DANIEL FUMBLED in his pocket for a condom, while Sophia shoved his jeans down around his hips. She was almost out of her mind with need despite the fact he'd just brought her to an earth-shattering orgasm that was still rippling through her body. She needed him to be inside of her. *Now.* His strong palm curled under her thigh and lifted it high once he had rolled a condom on. His eyes lifted and caught hers. For a moment, he held still, the head of his cock resting at her entrance. That single moment sent flames roaring through her, the need to be one with him ran so deep she could hardly bear it. Just when she thought he'd give in to what she needed and fill her, he dragged his cock back and forth in her slick folds with each pass sending streaks of pleasure through her.

When a moan broke from her throat, he leaned forward swiftly and caught her lips in a searing kiss. He pulled away with a growl when she arched her hips into him. Lost in his dark gaze, she gasped in relief when he finally sank into her. He plunged in deeply and lifted her knee higher. She curled her legs around his hips and held on when he started to move. He didn't hold back and surged into her in long, deep, pounding strokes. The door rattled behind her. He held her easily in his arms as he drummed into her, notching her higher and higher, pressure gathering in a wild storm inside. Another climax tore through her, a hoarse cry following. With a low growl, he surged into her one last time, his body going rigid and then shuddering. His head fell to her shoulder. Their breath came in mingled gasps as he held her against him.

He slowly lifted his head and adjusted his hold on her

before stepping away from the door and carrying her into the bathroom. He nudged the light on with his elbow and reached into the shower with one hand to turn it on, all the while holding her firmly against him. She didn't ever want him to let go. A small corner of her was terrified at the depth of feeling he elicited. The rest of her simply wanted to savor the feeling. He slowly eased his hold on her hips, and she slid down his body. He quickly disposed of his condom and tugged her into the shower with him.

A while later, she rested beside Daniel in bed. Daisy was snoring audibly at the foot of the bed. Sophia's palm was resting on Daniel's chest, and she could feel the slow and steady beat of his heart. His arm curled around her, resting on the curve of her hip to hold her close. A sense of deep comfort stole over her as she drifted off to sleep.

10

Daniel followed Sophia into her parents' home. After he'd dropped her off at work this morning, she'd texted him to ask if he wanted to talk with her mother this afternoon. He paused on the porch of the farmhouse and turned to look out over the small valley nearby. The sun glinted off a small stream winding through the corner of the valley. A mountain ridge rose tall on the far side, shading a cluster of aspen. A magpie burst out of the trees at the side of the house and swooped to land on the porch railing within arms length of Daniel. He heard the door opening and turned to face it. The woman who must be Sophia's mother gave Sophia a quick hug and stepped to Daniel, her smile beaming. She had dark hair streaked with silver and warm brown eyes. She wore a flowing skirt of gauzy green fabric that twirled around her ankles. She'd paired the skirt with a loose white blouse. Hammered silver hoops swung at her ears, and silver bracelets jangled as she reached for his hands and squeezed them.

"You must be Daniel. I'm Lila Ashworth, Sophia's

mother. It's so good to have you here in Painter." Her eyes were warm. Daniel felt as if she could see right through him.

"It's good to be here. Thank you for having me."

Lila loosened her hands when the magpie on the railing started chattering. It appeared as if the bird was speaking to her. She released Daniels' hands entirely and put her hands on her hips, eyeing the magpie. "Oh really? I already gave you one snack today."

Daniel glanced to Sophia who grinned and shrugged. The magpie chattered again and pecked at the railing. Lila stepped to the door beside which there was a decorative copper bucket with a lid. She reached inside and came out with a handful of cracked corn. She proceeded to feed the magpie who pecked daintily from her hand.

Lila glanced to Daniel and chuckled. "This is my friend Nina. She's been hanging around our house for the last few years."

Sophia caught his eye. "My mother feeds any animal that shows up. I hope you're hungry because I'm sure she's got something ready for us too."

Lila sprinkled the remaining cracked corn on the railing and gestured for them to follow her inside. Daniel looked around once he was seated at the table by the windows. The kitchen was warm and inviting with plants hanging in the windows, the scent of fresh baked bread, and Lila's warm presence as she puttered around getting a tray of sandwiches ready for them, along with making a fresh pot of coffee. She swatted Sophia away when she offered to help. Sophia sat down across from him and shrugged. "My mother's kind of bossy when it comes to her kitchen."

He grinned. "My mother was the same way." Lila stepped into the pantry, and he took that moment to reach across the table and tuck a loose lock of hair behind

Sophia's ear. He couldn't resist the excuse to touch her. Her cheeks turned a soft shade of pink. His chest tightened with emotion. Damn. Sophia hit him hard in more ways than one. He wanted her fiercely in the physical sense, but she'd also snaked her way straight into his heart and elicited a deep need to take care of her. She unsettled him because in record time, he found himself picturing her as a permanent part of his life. His confidence in this notion was absolute. His mother had warned him his shifter side would be possessive when it came to finding a mate. She'd told him once he found the right woman, he would know without a doubt she was meant to be his. He hadn't quite believed it, but now he'd met Sophia, it was hard to deny the truth of what she said.

Sophia's eyes were on his, the green darkening. The air around them felt heated, as if by the sheer power of need burning between them. *Not the time and place, man. Get a handle on yourself.* He took a breath and tore his eyes away. He curled his hand around the mug of coffee Lila had poured for him and took a gulp. He scrambled to rein in the lust galloping through his body. When it came to Sophia, he was helpless in a way he'd never experienced. He was used to being in control and having no trouble maintaining it. With her, all she had to do was exist, and it shook his hold on himself.

Lila walked out of the pantry and set the napkins in her hand on the tray and carried it over to the table, setting it in the center. "There you go. Help yourself," she said with a warm smile and nod to Daniel.

Over the next hour or so, Lila kindly answered any questions he had about his family. Beyond offering the bare bones of a family tree, she shared her memories of his mother when she was younger. When it came to talking about his family after David died, she was kind and careful. "I'm not sure how much you know about what happened."

"My mom told me David was shot and killed when he shifted at a playground," Daniel offered bluntly. "I know it was awful, but I've had a long time to adjust to his death. Oddly, I think it was probably better I didn't really understand what happened until I was older. It would have been so confusing. I was only three when he died."

Lila reached over and squeezed his hand quickly. "It was a tragedy. Plain and simple. The kind of accident that could happen to any young shifter. It's hard to learn how to control shifting until you're older. Your family was understandably devastated. To this day, I wish your parents hadn't moved away. They cut themselves off from anyone who could really understand what they were going through."

"I know. I've thought the same thing since I understood what happened. Nothing to be done about it now. Do you know much about my uncle?"

Lila was quiet for a long moment. She took a sip of coffee, her eyes thoughtful. "Nelson didn't take the situation well. It would have been hard for anyone. With your mother gone and your grandparents all but recluses at their old farm, he got bitter. I used to see him around town a lot more. He used to work at one of the mechanic shops in Painter. He was always out at Quinn's and a few other bars. He became a heavy drinker and a hard partier. Then, the last five years or so, he just kind of faded away. I see him every so often. I don't even know what he does for work. If you ask, he says odd jobs, but no one seems to know what those are. Your grandparents were pretty comfortable financially. Your grandfather made money in the logging industry and sold off some land before he died. His logging business owned properties all around Colorado and in other states. I don't know the exact details, but the lawyer who drew up your grandparents' will told me they tied up the money for your inheritance because they were concerned Nelson would burn through it. I have no idea how he's getting by."

Daniel now had more questions about his uncle. While Lila could offer much more about what led Nelson to the point he was at now, she was as puzzled as he was when it came to Nelson's current situation. "I have no idea what he's doing either. He didn't have much to say to me when I stopped by to introduce myself. He mentioned that my grandparents' old home was deeded to me after he passed away. Honestly, I didn't feel comfortable asking him too many questions."

"I can find that out for you. Your grandparents' attorney is a friend of mine. He'll want to know you're here. Maybe I can bring you by to meet him. Would you like that?"

"That would be great. Maybe he can fill me in on everything Nelson chose not to." Daniel finished his coffee and sat for a moment. "I really appreciate you taking time to talk with me about my family. It's sad to see how Nelson's turned out, but I suppose he didn't have it too easy after what happened."

Lila shook her head sharply. "It wasn't easy on anyone in your family, but it's no excuse for Nelson to be so cold to you. If I knew him better, I'd give him piece of my mind."

Daniel shrugged. "No need. Even though my parents passed away and I miss them, I was blessed to have two parents who loved me. It would have been nice to find an uncle, or any family, I could connect with and get to know, but it's okay. I'm glad I got to hear about them from you."

Lila's eyes crinkled at the corners when she smiled. "I'll see what I can find about some of your cousins. I know your mother had a few who lived in nearby areas."

At that, Lila stood up and went to refill her own cup of coffee. She held the coffee pot up and gestured to them. "More?"

Sophia shook her head. "I've got to get going. Daisy needs her dinner soon."

A few minutes later, Daniel watched Sophia hug her mother and was then enveloped in a warm hug from Lila himself. She pecked him on the cheek. "So good to meet you. I'll get back to you about meeting that attorney, okay?"

At that, she shooed them off the porch and watched while they drove away. Daniel glanced over at Sophia, wondering if he was going too far or too fast if he hoped to stay with her again tonight. The truth was, the idea of *not* being with her tonight bordered on painful.

SOPHIA FORCED herself to keep her eyes on the winding road ahead of her. Her body was humming at Daniel's nearness. He'd been quiet since they left her parents' house. Her mind spun in circles. She was startled by how quickly her heart had become entangled in Daniel. She hadn't doubted her attraction to him, but she hadn't expected it to grow by leaps and bounds, or for him to so effortlessly knock down the barriers she kept in place around her heart. With Daniel, she felt as if she was diving off a cliff—that's how hard and fast she was falling. To complicate matters, she didn't know how he viewed her and if he felt the depth of connection she did.

In the enclosed space of her car, she could feel every breath he took. The air around them felt electric. The sun had fallen behind the mountains, leaving the wispy light of dusk in its wake. Shadows of trees fell across the road as they drove toward her house. Daniel had driven over to meet her, and they left from there to go see her mother. She wanted to ask him to stay. Again. Yet, she worried she was being too forward. Her mind started running through the long list of reasons why now was not a good time to try to start a relationship. Odd thing was she kept trying to tell herself the main reason was because she needed to be there for her family, but her mind kept whispering that it wasn't that. *You're afraid because you've never felt like this. With anyone. Maybe your reasons made sense before, but now you're just scared.* She sighed mentally and tried to stop chasing her thoughts in circles.

Daniel's voice knocked her yammering mind off its loop. "Thanks for taking me to meet your mother."

She slowed and came to a stop at an intersection. She glanced over, her eyes colliding with his. It felt as if a flame licked its way through the air between them, coiling in a circle around them. She forgot what he said for a moment, belatedly realizing she should reply. "Oh sure," she managed over the pounding of her heart. Pure need coursed through her as she looked over at him. Another car approached the intersection, its headlights illuminating the inside of her car. She jerked her eyes away from Daniel and drove through the intersection and turned onto her road. A moment later, she parked her car in the driveway. She didn't know if it was the smart thing to do, but she didn't want Daniel to leave just yet, so she ignored her doubts, kicking them to the back of her mind.

"Do you want to come in? Daisy would love to see you."

For God's sake, you're telling him your dog would love to see him. How about just admitting you want to see him?

She caught herself just before she was about to shake her head. Daniel glanced her way. "I'd love to see Daisy, but that's not why I'd like to come in," he said bluntly.

A wash of heat rushed through her, flushing her inside and out. "Oh. Okay." Flustered, she turned her car off and fumbled to unbuckle her seat belt. Seconds later, she was standing beside her car. He climbed out and walked at her side up the steps. When they reached the front door, she took a breath and turned to face him. If he was going to be straight with her, she wasn't going to be a coward with him.

"Daisy will be glad to see you, but I wanted you to come in because I didn't want you to go yet."

Her pulse leapt wildly, and butterflies thronged in her belly. She was relieved she'd simply stated the truth and terrified at the same time. His eyes met hers in the soft glow cast from her porch light, his gaze dark and intent. "It's good to know I'm not alone in this." His words came out rough and raw.

She reached up and curled her hand around his neck, tugging him down to meet her for a quick kiss. When she broke away, she whispered against his lips. "You're not alone." She looked into the blur of his gaze, the connection between them live and pulsing. Her heart clenched and warmth curled around it.

Unsettled, she turned away and unlocked the front door, flicking on the lights as she entered. Daisy was waiting for them and immediately circled them both, nudging her head against their hands for greetings. Sophia went straight to the kitchen and got Daisy's food ready. Once Daisy was eating, Sophia glanced to Daniel who was seated at the kitchen table.

"I'm not really up for cooking. Would you mind takeout again? We could do pizza or something else."

"Pizza is perfect," he replied firmly.

She snagged the menu off the refrigerator and handed it to him. "You pick."

He shrugged and didn't even bother looking. "Let's do the half and half thing we did last time."

Sophia tugged her phone out and called in the order. Once that was done, she became instantly restless. The pulse of need she felt for Daniel was so strong, it was hard to ignore. Daisy finished eating and promptly curled up on her dog bed in the living room.

Sophia leaned against the counter, crossing her arms as if she could somehow contain the beat of desire thrumming through her. Daniel stood up from the table and walked to stand in front of her. He rested his palms on the counter on either side of her. The air around them felt charged. Heat suffused her when she met his eyes—dark and intent, focused solely on her. She felt as if she was the center of his universe in that moment. He was the center of hers. The moment was taut with need, fraught with the depth of sheer want between them. He dipped his head and fit his mouth over hers. In seconds, their kiss exploded, a fierce meeting of lips and tongues.

He stepped closer and slid a hand up her back, pulling her flush against him. The warmth of his palm sent an electric current racing up her spine. He tore his mouth free when she gasped. His lips dusted over her face before traveling down her neck, nipping and licking his way over the sensitive skin. She could feel the heat of his shaft resting against her and arched into it. He slid a knee between her thighs and slipped his hand under the hem of her t-shirt. The calloused skin of his palm stroked up the curve of her belly, striking sparks along the surface of her skin. Hot, liquid need built in her center. Her panties dampened as he nudged her knee against her. Pleasure arced sharply through her with each nudge of his knee. She needed more. Now.

She tore at his jeans, yanking the buttons free and curling her palm around the thick, hard length of his cock. His breath hissed through his teeth. She put a palm on his chest and pushed back swiftly and firmly before shimmying down as she hooked her hands over his jeans and briefs and shoved them down around his hips.

"Sophia..." Her name fell roughly from his lips.

She ignored him and stroked her hand up and down his cock before drawing her tongue along the underside.

Several long, slow licks and a low groan came from him. She closed her mouth around him, drawing him deep. His cock throbbed and pulsed as she stroked him in her wet grip. He gasped her name again. When she paused and glanced up, he reached down and lifted her roughly. He shoved her leggings down with one hand and dragged his fingers roughly across the damp silk of her panties. The need to feel him inside her was so great, it clawed at her.

In a rush, she turned into his touch as he curled a palm around to cup her bottom, squeezing roughly. She scrambled to grip the edge of the counter as she pushed her hips back into him. She felt the brush of his hard shaft against her, the skin hot and velvety. One palm stroked roughly up her back, threading into her hair, while the other shoved her panties out of the way. She felt him fumble and heard the tear of foil before he rolled a condom on. He paused for a brief moment, the head of his cock resting against her. In one swift surge, he sank inside deeply.

She arched back into the delicious stretch. She needed fast and hard, needed him to slake the lust coursing through her. He gave her precisely what she needed, stroking deeply, again and again and again. He gripped her hair, tugging her into each thrust. They moved in a circle of surges, each one driving deeper. Pressure gathered inside, spinning tighter and tighter until it spun loose, sending sharp streaks of pleasure spiraling outward. She cried out hoarsely as her climax crashed through her. Daniel suddenly went rigid and drove deep one last time before a emitting a low growl as he shuddered against her.

His hand loosened in her hair and slowly slid down her spine, his touch anchoring her, bringing her back to herself. She turned her head to the side, her cheek resting on the cool tile counter. After several long moments, the only sound the deep gusts of their breathing, headlights flashed through the front windows.

"I think that might be our pizza," Daniel said, his voice low and gravelly.

She flushed to realize she'd lost herself so completely in Daniel she forgot they were expecting someone to show up any minute. She giggled as Daniel slowly pulled away, his hand squeezing her hip softly. He quickly disposed of the condom in the trash. They both straightened their clothes. Daniel stepped to her side just as the doorbell rang. He cupped her cheek and dropped a lingering kiss on her lips. When he pulled back, his eyes held hers. "Just so you know, you drive me wild," he whispered.

At that, he turned away and strode to the door. While he paid for the pizza and exchanged friendly conversation with the delivery guy, she stood frozen in the kitchen, her fingers on her lips as if she could hold his touch there. The sound of the front door closing knocked her back into awareness. She dropped her hand and went to get plates out. She was filling their wineglasses when he walked back into the kitchen holding the pizza aloft. Daisy ambled along behind him and immediately sat at his feet by the table.

Hours later, they were lounging on the couch with the evening news on. The local late night news came on and announced a recent arrest of another local drug dealer. Daniel's arm was curled over her shoulders and her legs were thrown across his lap. Daisy was on his other side, occupying most of the couch, with her head resting on Sophia's calves. Daniel idly stroked her shoulder. "Hard to believe there's problems with drugs around here."

Sophia canted her eyes to the side, catching his. She considered for a moment if she should tell him of the shifter smuggling scandal in Painter and its threat to the secrecy that had kept them safe for centuries. Shifters were on tenterhooks of fear that if it was somehow discovered shifters were smuggling and how, it would expose them in the worst possible light. Though she hadn't quite accepted how well Daniel could read her, he could. In a brief glance, she saw that he sensed her concern. She took a breath and let it out.

"There's problems with drugs everywhere, but in Painter it's an ugly shifter problem. You might as well hear it from me. I'll try to keep it brief. A few years back, there were rumors that some shifters started smuggling drugs for money. I mean, a perfect cover really. Mountain lions are known for stealth and for staying out of sight. A shifter could cover a lot of ground and no one would think twice about even looking into it. Next thing you know, it balloons and we hear rumors about smuggling as far as away as Montana and even Maine. Catamount is the original shifter community back in Maine. They took down the local leaders there and pretty much shut it down. A few other areas have done their best to deal with it, but we haven't had much luck here. Only low level dealers have been arrested, but the network keeps popping back up. Whoever's pulling the strings has money and time to keep funding it and recruiting more shifters. The whole thing makes me sick. I hate talking about it because being a shifter is sacred, it's an honor. These guys are bringing dishonor on all of us and putting us at risk. If shifters are officially discovered, it could make life nearly impossible for us."

Daniel's eyes widened as she spoke. He sat quietly for several beats after she finished. With a sigh, he ran a hand through his hair. "Well, damn. That's a hell of a mess," he said bluntly.

A wash of anger knotted in her chest as she considered the mess a small brush with the drugs floating through Painter had left for her brother. Logically, she knew damn well Heath was fully responsible for his choice to try to seek out illegal methods to manage his addiction to painkillers. But she was angry. Angry at the whims of fate that resulted in the car accident that put Heath in so much pain, angry at the doctors who didn't make sure he had the support he needed when they started to wean him off of painkillers, and angry at the easy access to drugs in Painter with thanks to the shifters who brought them here.

Daniel's eyes narrowed with concern. He angled his head to the side. "Is there something else?"

She sighed. "It's a bit of a sore subject because of what happened to my brother."

Daniel's thumb stroked in a slow circle on her shoulder. He waited quietly. She took a gulp of air and quickly summarized the series of events that led to Heath's arrest for trying to score heroin. "I mean, we had no idea how addictive those damn painkillers were. The doctors said they would decrease the dosage slowly to help wean him off, but it wasn't enough. He had withdrawal symptoms. It was that bad. I'm not saying the way he chose to handle it was smart. It was stupid. Completely stupid. The only good thing that came out of it is he got the help he needed. He's healthy and healing now. But the whole thing makes me sick. I don't think he'd ever have gone the route he did if it wasn't so damn easy."

She had looked away, staring blindly at the television, while she recited Heath's story. At the sound of Daniel's voice, she turned to him, his face coming into sharp focus —the strong, angled planes, his dark brows, his navy eyes holding her in their gaze with warmth and understanding. "He's had a rough year. Your whole family has. I'd be damn angry too."

The knot of anger loosened in her chest. She shrugged and tried to smile, but it wobbled. Daniel stroked a hand through her hair. "You don't have to try to make it seem okay. It's not."

She shook her head. "No, it's not. It's been a long, shitty year." She took a breath, letting it out slowly. "Vivi and I have been doing some scouting around. We think we found a cabin where the smugglers are meeting."

His hand stilled in her hair. When she glanced at him, his features were tight. She sensed he was concerned and was holding himself back. "Go ahead. You probably want to tell me to be careful and back off. No need. Heath already gave me that lecture."

"Oh? What'd he have to say?"

"He told me to stay out of it. I'm not going to be stupid, but the police aren't getting anywhere, so we might as well see what we can find out. Vivi's a shifter too, so we can hold our own. We're not going to do anything but scout. If we get some good leads, we'll pass it on to the police."

Daniel leaned his head back on the couch. "I don't like it. I know we haven't known each other that long, but you mean a lot to me. A. Lot. I don't want to see you get hurt."

Her heart clenched at the protectiveness thrumming under his words. Every moment with him stitched her closer and closer to him, so close she didn't think she could consider anything other than being with him. He rolled his head to the side, his hand stroking through her hair again. "Promise me you'll be careful."

"Always. You could come with us, you know."

He considered for a moment before a smile slowly spread across his face. "Maybe I will."

11

———

Sophia took a bite of her burger just as Vivi approached the table where she was sitting with Daniel. After several nights of nothing but each other, they'd decided on dinner at Quinn's. As usual, Quinn's was bustling. The tables were filled and a local band was getting set up to play later that night.

Vivi tugged a chair out and sat down with a grin. "It's about damn time you showed up somewhere around town!"

Sophia finished chewing and took a sip of water. "I'm in town every day at Mile High. You know, the coffee shop I own?"

That got her an eye roll from Vivi. "That doesn't count. You've been holed up at home with your new lover boy here," she said, gesturing to Daniel with a sly grin.

Sophia flushed straight through. It wasn't that she was hiding anything about her and Daniel, but she wasn't used to being involved with anyone. Not to mention, he had her so hot and bothered all the time, she could hardly think straight. She took another bite of her burger to buy some time. Vivi turned her attention to Daniel.

"You've stolen my best friend, so you'd better be worth it."

Daniel choked on the bite of food he'd just swallowed. Vivi helpfully pounded him on the back and left him laughing by the end of it. He shrugged ruefully. "I haven't stolen her, as you say. I just happen to like spending time with her. A lot."

Vivi's eyes widened. Her gaze bounced between them. "Well then. If you adore her as she should be adored, then it's okay. If you harm a hair on her head or even cause her the slightest pain, I'll make your life hell." She jabbed her finger at him and then let her hand fall. "You seem like a good guy though, and she really likes you, so I'm sure we'll be fine," she finished sweetly.

Daniel looked from Vivi to Sophia, as if unsure how to respond.

"She's more bark than bite," Sophia offered.

"Okay," he said carefully.

Vivi burst out laughing. "I can't help it. I have to make sure you know the deal, but no need to worry. I see the way you look at her."

Daniel wasn't bothered by her observation and shrugged, his eyes lingering possessively on Sophia.

"Okay, enough of this. Moving on. How about we go for a hike tomorrow?" Vivi asked, turning to Sophia.

Going for a hike meant walking far enough into the woods to shift and taking off to scout. Sophia had filled Vivi in on her conversation with Daniel the other night. She looked to him and then Vivi again. "Sounds good. Daniel might want to join us. Any news?"

Vivi shrugged. "Maybe. I have some ideas. I'll fill you in on the drive out tomorrow. Okay?"

At Sophia's nod, conversation moved on. Vivi was still sitting with them a while later when Heath walked into the restaurant. When his eyes landed on them, he headed straight for their table. "Hey, hey! I was hoping to find you here." He leaned over and quickly hugged Sophia before turning to Vivi.

Vivi stood up and threw her arms around him. "No half-ass side hug for me. You've been gone too long."

Heath chuckled as she stepped away and sat back down. "Mind if I join you?" he asked, catching Sophia's eyes.

"Go right ahead." She gestured to Daniel. "This is Daniel. Daniel, this is Heath. He's my one and only brother," she said pointing to Heath as he sat down.

Daniel and Heath shook hands across the table and exchanged greetings. Sophia savored the next little while. It felt like such a luxury to have her brother home and looking healthy and strong again. She'd wanted an opportunity for him to meet Daniel and this chance meeting eased the introduction. Heath was a typical older brother with the edge of a shifter. He could be overprotective if he sensed anything off kilter with any man interested in her. Since she'd yet to have much of a serious relationship, she'd been worrying over how he might respond to Daniel. She knew she couldn't hide how much Daniel meant to her. With Vivi here as a buffer of sorts, they easily got to talking.

Sophia and Daniel left Quinn's later. Daniel looped his arm over her shoulder as they walked outside. The air was chilly as summer evenings in the mountains tended to be. When she shivered, he tugged her closer, and she savored the warmth emanating from him. They reached his car, and he held the door for her. Once he'd walked around and started the car, he glanced over at her, his eyes intent.

"I'm hoping it's okay if I stay with you tonight."

As if she could contemplate anything else. She nodded and considered they hadn't really talked much about what was happening between them. Meanwhile, desire galloped forward, tangling with emotions running unchecked and driven by a force of their own. In a blink of time, Daniel had woven himself deeply into her heart and body. She couldn't imagine life without him now. She'd always heard this was how it would be when she met her mate, but she hadn't quite realized the depth of power the connection could hold over her. Its power was so strong, part of her wanted to push back against it, while another part of her simply wanted to surrender to it.

He was watching and waiting. She cleared her throat. "We, uh, haven't really talked about us."

"No, we haven't." His words fell softly in the quiet of his car. "Do we need to talk?"

She pondered his question. "I don't know. I don't know how you feel…"

His words cut across hers. "I want you. Now and forever."

Her heart soared. It was as if he'd thrown open a window into her heart and light and fresh air were pouring in. Her body set to humming, as it did whenever he was near.

Though she couldn't seem for speak, her expression must have shown him how she was feeling because he leaned over and dragged the backs of his fingers along her jawline before tracing her lips. Goosebumps prickled in the wake of his touch. He caught her lips in a fierce, swift kiss before pulling back just as swiftly. Without a word, he started the car and drove to her house.

~

THE FOLLOWING AFTERNOON, she and Vivi hiked into the woods with Daniel. She'd never shifted with him, so she wasn't certain how this would feel. In a way, she was relieved Vivi was with them. It would ease any awkwardness. She didn't doubt her feelings for Daniel, or his for her, but it was all so much and so intense. When they reached the stream where they usually shifted, Vivi glanced between them, her eyes holding on Daniel.

"All we're doing is looking. We'll head to the bluff where we saw the shifters last time and see if we can get a little closer."

Daniel nodded. "Lead the way."

In a flash, they shifted. Vivi bounded ahead. Sophia paused for a moment and looked Daniel over. In lion form, he was strong, lean and muscled, just as he was in human form. He held himself proudly. In a way, the fact he didn't learn about his shifter side until he was older almost made him purer. He wasn't weighted down by expectations. He simply was... a glorious specimen of cat. His fur was on the dark side, the golden tipped with a hue of brown. He caught her eyes and flicked his tail before stretching and leaping to follow Vivi. Sophia followed swiftly, weaving between the trees to catch up quickly.

They ran quietly through the forest, making their way further up into the mountains. Vivi slowed to a stop well inside the tree line before they reached the bluff overlooking the valley where the cabin was. Sophia scented mountain lions and humans in the distance, once again a clear indicator shifters were nearby. The three cats walked in almost silence to the edge of the trees. Vivi nudged her head forward, indicating for Sophia and Daniel to position themselves in the shelter of one of the boulders on the bluff, while she headed to another boulder with a different angle of sight over the small valley.

The old cabin came into view when Sophia carefully glanced around the corner of the boulder. Daniel, with his greater height, was able to look above the boulder. The sight of him in lion form took her breath away. She tore her eyes away and looked out over the valley. The ground outside the cabin showed evidence of recent traffic with the dusty ground crisscrossed in tracks. As they watched, a man came out of the cabin and walked to lean against a fence in front of the cabin. She sensed Daniel stiffen, but she didn't dare move, so she held still. Long moments later, two mountain lions appeared on the far side of the valley and began to cross into the open field by the cabin. Suddenly, one of the cats stopped, lifting its nose in the air. Sophia canted her eyes toward Vivi who was in her line of sight, so she could catch her eyes without turning. Vivi shook her head, the barest movement.

After a slow perusal of the valley, the lion who'd stopped began moving again. The cats followed the man into the cabin. After several taut moments, Sophia tossed her head and started backing into the trees. Vivi followed, although Daniel remained for a long moment, his eyes traversing back and forth across the valley. She and Vivi waited quietly. He finally turned and ambled back into the trees. The strength and power emanating from him was immense.

Suddenly the scent of another lion gusted on the breeze. Sophia locked eyes with Vivi. Whoever this lion was, he was getting closer to them and was most definitely male. Daniel's head lifted and turned slowly. In lion form, just as in human form, he was larger than the average male and heavily muscled. She didn't doubt he could hold his own in a fight if need be, but she didn't want him to be forced into a confrontation. The problem was if they could smell the other lion, the lion could smell them and would likely be upon them at any moment if he felt threatened.

Sophia hoped numbers were on their side. In seconds, the lion came into view at the edge of the trees. She was uncertain who it was. Among shifters, they could recognize each other if they knew each other. Painter's shifter community was close-knit, but she didn't personally know every shifter. Over the years, the population of shifters had grown as well. The lion held still for a tense moment before dashing straight for Daniel with a roar. Daniel held his position and caught the other lion in his teeth by the neck as the lion attempted to attack. Snarls and growls echoed through the trees. Daniel quickly and clearly dominated the other lion, although the lion wasn't giving up without a fierce fight.

Just when Sophia thought perhaps it was only one mountain lion, another appeared in the edge of the forest and made straight for her and Vivi. In a flash, the lion was upon them. She and Vivi had grown up tussling together with each other and other cats, so they were accustomed to joining forces in a fight. They easily knocked the other cat off his feet. He was swift and bounded back up with a roar.

She loved the power that rushed through her in a fight. Adrenaline rolled through her in waves as she swiped at the lion and caught the ruff of his neck in her teeth. In minutes, they pinned the cat. She tasted the iron of his blood in her mouth. Vivi's paw held the lion down. She nudged Sophia's shoulder. Sophia followed Vivi's eyes to see Daniel had pinned the other cat.

Steam rose around them in the damp air of the forest from the collective heaves of the lions on the heels of a fight. The lion beneath them shifted. It was a man she didn't recognize. In the moments following, the other lion shifted as well. Two stranger shifters stood amongst them, battered and bruised. They were silent and sullen on the trek out of the forest.

~

HOURS LATER, after a long hike back in human form, they pulled up at the police station. Sophia knew several of the cops were shifters, so they'd called ahead and arranged for one to meet them.

Roger Shaw met them at the door and quickly escorted them inside. Another officer, Brad Hall, escorted the two shifters through the waiting room into the back. After Sophia introduced Daniel, Roger leaned back in his desk. "Sounds like you and Vivi stumbled across the same place we've been keeping an eye on."

Vivi crossed her arms and glared at Roger. "Well, maybe if you'd been giving us some updates on things we wouldn't feel like we had to look into things ourselves."

Roger ran a hand through his dark hair and chuckled. They'd grown up with Roger. He was an old family friend and solid as they came. His brown eyes caught Sophia's. "Heath know you've been scouting around?"

"He's not too thrilled about it." She felt defensive and argumentative at once. "Look, Heath's been through hell, and I'm pissed about what these guys have done to Painter. No one knows who to trust anymore, and it feels like nothing is getting anywhere. We need to find out who's involved and shut it down!"

Roger sighed. "I'm sorry. I get why you're doing this, but trust me when I say we're working on it. Finding these guys will help. I'm guessing they've probably scented us before when we've been out there, but they have enough sense to steer clear since they know who we are. They probably decided to take you all on, thinking they could hold their own. They obviously don't know you and Vivi can fight with the best of us."

He caught Daniel's eyes. "Nice to meet you by the way. I'm glad you were there."

Daniel nodded. "I haven't had a chance to mention this, but I think I know the man we saw."

Roger's eyes narrowed, while Sophia and Vivi swung to him.

"Why didn't you say something?" Vivi asked impatiently.

Daniel was unruffled. "Because we had those two guys with us the whole way back, and I didn't want to clue them in. Anyway, it makes me sick to say this, but I think it's my uncle."

"Nelson Weaver?" Roger asked.

"Yup. We didn't have a great view, but I'm pretty damn sure. I've only met him once since I got to Painter, but it wouldn't surprise me to find out he was involved. My gut tells me he's up to no good. There's also the fact I can't figure out what he's doing for work." He caught Sophia's eyes. "Sophia's mother told me my grandparents tied up their inheritance, so he's not living off that. The house is mostly unused, and he's damn cagey about what he's doing to get by."

"You really think the man was your uncle?" Sophia asked, reaching for Daniel's hand.

He squeezed her hand and nodded. "Think so." He took a breath and looked back to Roger.

Roger nodded thoughtfully. "Nelson's been on our list of possibilities ever since this smuggling ring got started. He's skirted the edge of the law for years. Usually small stuff, but he's always looking for quick cash and an easy way out."

The conversation carried on with Roger asking Daniel questions about anything he might have seen out at his grandparents' old property. By the time they left, darkness was falling. Between the long afternoon and early evening, Sophia was weary. They dropped Vivi off and returned to her house. Daisy greeted them enthusiastically at the door.

She quickly fed Daisy and turned to Daniel. "I'm starving, but I need a shower."

Without a word, Daniel curled his palm around her hand and led her through the living room, into her bedroom and into the bathroom.

12

Steam filled the air, light haloing through the soft mist. Sophia stood in the shower, rinsing the soap out of her hair. She bore several scratches on her back and shoulders, one angry and red. The fight in the forest had brought Daniel's feelings for her into sharp focus. Seeing her fight so wildly and fiercely had driven deep into his being. He recalled again how his mother had described how he'd feel when he met his mate. She'd kept saying it was hard for a human to understand because it was so primal. Sophia in lion form had called to him so strongly, he only wanted to claim her.

He ran a hand over her shoulder and down her back, carefully tracing the deep scratch. She turned to face him, running her hands over her hair, the water cascading around her. His body tensed, wracked with longing. Lust rolled through him, a hot rumble. Her hands fell to his shoulders and stroked down his arms. He caught her lips in his, moving swiftly. He hooked a hand under her thigh and lifted it. He stroked a finger into her folds, finding her ready and waiting. She whispered against his lips. "I'm on the pill...just so you know."

He pulled back a fraction and opened his eyes. "Are you...?"

"I'm sure."

He didn't wait and positioned his cock at her entrance. He cupped her cheek and held her gaze as he surged into her. Her breath broke on a low moan. He moved swiftly, claiming her fully and completely. Their coupling was fast and fierce. In moments, she was throbbing around him, her body arching and shuddering as she cried out. His orgasm ripped through him, his release so thorough, he had to brace a hand against the shower wall to keep from falling.

A while later, they lounged on the couch with Daisy stretched out on the floor at their feet. Too weary to cook, they'd ordered takeout from Quinn's. Sophia had a plate on her lap and was nibbling on sweet potato fries when she glanced over. "You don't seem too upset about your uncle."

He shrugged. "I'm not happy, but it didn't surprise me. It's just hard idea to wrap my brain around. Sure, I hoped I'd come here and find some family and it would be a good thing. Nelson isn't a happy guy. Even if he wasn't involved in drug smuggling, it was pretty damn clear he and I weren't going to have much of a relationship. I can't say one hundred percent it was him, but I'm as sure as I can be. We'll see what happens. I'm damn relieved you finally talked to the police about what you and Vivi saw."

Sophia sighed. "We always said we would if we had something worthwhile."

"Two shifters picking a fight is your standard for worthwhile?"

She rolled her eyes. "Whatever." Her expression sobered. "I'm sorry you came all the way here and found an uncle who's not exactly there for you."

He looked over at her, her dark hair tumbling loosely

around her shoulders, her gorgeous green eyes, the arch of her brow, and the soft curve of her cheekbone. He lifted a hand and brushed a loose lock of hair off her forehead. "I found you," he said, his chest tightening with emotion.

She curled her hand around his and squeezed it.

The moment was interrupted when Daisy sat up and nudged her nose on the couch between them. Sophia laughed softly and freed her hand to stroke Daisy's head. He cleared his throat. "Even with everything that happened with my brother, you should know I had a happy childhood. My parents loved me. Maybe things were mixed up because of how afraid they were after how David died, but I didn't come here looking for something I never had. I had loving parents who did their best under difficult circumstances. I came here mostly to find out about the shifter side of myself. My mother loved Painter and missed it, so I wanted to see the place she loved so much. Don't worry about me because of Nelson. If he's involved, I'd prefer he's held accountable."

Still stroking Daisy's head, Sophia smiled softly. "Okay." She snagged another sweet potato fry and nibbled on it before grabbing the remote and flicking on the television.

Sophia sat on Vivi's porch with Jax twining himself around her ankles, purring so loudly he practically made her vibrate. Vivi was braiding Julianna's hair. She tied an elastic band around the end of one braid and started on the other side.

"So, it's obvious you're head over heels for Daniel and he all but slobbers whenever he looks at you. What now?" Vivi asked.

Sophia watched Vivi's hands smoothly weave Julianna's dark hair into a tidy braid. She glanced up into Vivi's sharp gaze. It was a fair question, but she didn't know what the answer was. She shrugged. "I'm not sure." *Don't be silly. You're sure. You know exactly what he means to you. Maybe so, and that's half the problem.* She wasn't sure she was ready to make Daniel a permanent part of her life.

As usual, Vivi didn't mince words. "Soph, you're either playing dumb, or you're about to let the man who's clearly meant to be yours drift away because you're too proud to admit what's obvious to anyone who sees you two together."

The sound of an elastic band snapping onto Julianna's other braid punctuated Vivi's words. She lifted Julianna's two braids high in the air and let them fall. "All done!" Julianna whirled around and planted a noisy kiss on her mother's cheek before running down the steps into the yard to play. Vivi leaned back in her chair and caught Sophia's eyes.

Sophia sighed. "That obvious, huh?"

Vivi's gaze softened. "We're shifters. If we find the right one, it's usually obvious. Daniel's the one for you. It doesn't really matter whether you planned on it, or you're too busy." She paused, her eyes considering. "I know you. I know you've been hyper-focused on your family and taking care of everyone. Heath is fine now. You can still be there for him and make room in your life for Daniel."

Sophia's stomach churned with the familiar worry she'd carried inside ever since Heath's accident. She was always waiting for the next thing to go wrong and bracing herself to be prepared. She knew Vivi was right. Vivi knew her probably better than she knew herself sometimes. Daniel had come out of nowhere. The intensity and depth of her feelings for him was almost overpowering. The sheer strength of it in such a short time knocked her off kilter.

She smiled ruefully at Vivi. "How do you know me so well?"

Vivi grinned. "Same reason you know me so well. You're the friend who told me to face up to the fact that Julianna's father was not the man I was trying to pretend he was. I wanted him to be what Daniel is to you. The fact I haven't heard from him in three years proved how wrong I was. So when I see the neon sign blinking over you and Daniel, I just want to make sure you don't ignore it."

A laugh bubbled out of Sophia. "Neon sign? What does it say?"

"For you. Don't be stupid just because you're busy," Vivi said, somehow keeping a completely straight face.

Sophia laughed so hard she couldn't catch her breath. When she finally stopped, she looked over at Vivi. "I'll do my best not to be stupid." She reached down and lifted Jax onto her lap.

Sophia leaned her hip against the counter at Mile High Grounds and took a sip of the espresso Tommy had just prepped for her. Though they offered a wide variety of specialized coffee drinks at Mile High, her personal favorite was straight espresso. Tommy had perfected it, and she turned to him with a smile as she lifted her small mug. "Excellent as always."

Tommy glanced up from the next coffee shot he was pulling from the espresso machine and winked. "Learned it from you."

She chuckled and savored another sip. It was late afternoon—the time of day when it wasn't quite afternoon or evening, but a magical in-between time when the light haloed everything in its soft glow. Her coffee shop had tall windows that allowed the sun to fall through in golden shafts through the room. This time of day was quiet. It was before the bustle of after work customers. At the moment, a number of customers were sitting quietly. Some were college students with their eyes glued to their laptops, either studying or typing away, presumably working on papers. A small cluster of women occupied a few tables in the corner. They comprised a loosely organized knitting group that came every week ostensibly to knit, although they mostly talked with yarn draped across their laps.

She waited on a few customers and glanced at the clock. Daniel had stayed at her house for the day to work. He'd all but abandoned his apartment, which was perfectly fine with her. She was doing her damnedest to follow Vivi's pointed advice and let herself enjoy Daniel. He didn't make assumptions and had asked about working from her place. He'd commented that his apartment was hardly home for him, while being at her house meant Daisy didn't have to spend the day alone. Daisy, of course, loved having Daniel around. Sophia could imagine Daisy simply parked herself at Daniel's feet wherever he happened to be working in the house. He'd texted a little while ago and said he'd be stopping by for a coffee. Even though her nights were spent with him, a few hours away and she was aflutter with anticipation to see him again.

The bell on the door rang. Sophia looked up and saw Heath entering. Just seeing him lately made her heart feel lighter. After a year of lugging around the weight of worry about him, seeing him back to his old self, even stronger, was such a gift tears sprang to her eyes. Heath glanced around as he made his way to the counter. He pushed his sunglasses up on his head when he reached her.

"Hey Soph. Thought I'd stop by for a coffee. How's it going?"

"It's going. What do you want for coffee?"

Heath's eyes perused the chalkboard menu on the wall above the counter. "What's that chocolate coffee thing I like?"

"A mocha latte. You want one of those?"

Heath nodded firmly. When she turned to pass the order on to Tommy, Tommy called out. "Already on it."

She turned back, and Heath was sliding several bills across the counter.

"You don't need to pay. This one's on me."

Heath ignored her and dropped the bills in the tip jar. "If you won't let me pay for it, then you get a fat tip."

The bell chimed again. When she glanced over reflexively, Daniel was walking through the door. Her belly clenched and heat slid through her veins at the mere sight of him. He was his usual tall, dark and sexy self. He wore faded jeans that rode low on his hips and a black t-shirt. His chiseled chest and abs filled out the t-shirt. She savored the flex of his muscles as his arms swung loosely at his sides while he walked toward the counter. His eyes locked on hers, and her breath hitched. She remembered her brother was standing right there and shook her head to knock her mind off the pure desire racing through her.

When Daniel reached the counter, he greeted Heath before leaning over and dropping a kiss on her cheek. She flushed straight through. Heath's eyes bounced between them, but he held his silence. Daniel leaned against the counter and slid his hands into his pockets. "I'm here for that coffee I mentioned," he said with a half-smile.

Her pulse skittered, but she managed to stay focused. "Right. Double shot Americano?"

He nodded firmly. As she turned toward Tommy, he handed Heath's coffee forward. "Heard the next one too," Tommy offered with a grin.

"I know. I forget I don't need to repeat everything for you."

When she turned back, Heath was asking Daniel what he did for work.

"I do freelance computer coding. I've done it for years. I

have a few contracts to provide tech support for some companies, but mostly I do coding for special projects."

"That makes it easy to work wherever you want. Not a bad gig," Heath commented.

"Works for me. I like it. The only part that's hard is it's pretty solitary work."

"I can see that. So what do you think of Painter now you've been here a little bit?"

"I like it." Daniel paused and glanced to Sophia. He turned back to Heath. "To be honest, I wasn't sure if I'd want to stay when I came out here. But now, I'm not planning on going anywhere."

Sophia's heart tightened. He meant for her to understand his intent. It was obvious Heath sensed as such. Heath's eyes narrowed and he glanced from Daniel to her. If Heath wanted to say anything, he elected not to. He simply nodded. "Well, I know Soph's glad to have you here."

Heath's eyes landed on her, and she could practically see the wheels turning in his head. She figured he may have an opinion, but he would keep it to himself for now. She interpreted his silence as approval. It might be grudging, but if Heath had a problem with Daniel, it would be clear even if he didn't say a word. The bell chimed again. This time Vivi strolled through, a wide smile gracing her face when she saw them. She made straight for the counter, putting herself right between Heath and Daniel. "Mocha latte, please," she said brightly.

"Coming right up," Tommy called out as he slid Daniel's drink forward.

Vivi glanced amongst everyone, her eyes lingering on Heath. She leaned up and pecked him quickly on the cheek. "It's so damn good to have you home."

The corner of Heath's mouth kicked up in a grin. "Damn good to be home. What's this I hear about you all being involved in the arrest of a couple of shifter smugglers?"

Vivi shrugged. "We were just checking things out. We didn't start anything, so don't blame us for that." She glanced to Sophia. "Roger was at Quinn's last night. He mentioned the two guys they have in custody decided it might be worthwhile to talk. He wouldn't tell me much of anything, but he did say he thinks the lead on Nelson was solid. He's hoping they might finally get enough info to get somewhere."

Heath's eyes narrowed. "Nelson? Nelson Weaver, your uncle?" he asked, turning to Daniel.

Daniel nodded and took a gulp of his coffee. "When we were out there, I thought he was the guy waiting at the cabin."

"You know much about him?" Heath asked.

"Not much beyond what my own mother shared and then your mother. My mother lost touch with Nelson years ago, so your mother actually had more up to date info. Even that wasn't much though. When I went out to meet him at my grandparents' old house, he wasn't exactly friendly."

Heath was quiet for a long moment before he shook his head sharply. "Now the police are on the trail, will you two back the hell off?"

"I said we would and we will," Sophia said quickly. "You can't blame us for wanting to. No one got hurt, so just let it go."

Heath's eyes were dark and somber. "Rumor has it there was s scuffle in the forest."

Vivi spoke up. "Maybe so, but it's not like we can't hold our own. Obviously we did, so don't turn this into something it wasn't."

Tension raced through Sophia. She understood Heath's concern, but she didn't think he quite grasped how much it mattered to them to find some chinks in the armor around the smuggling network. Without its existence in Painter and well-known easy access to drugs, Heath might have never even considered trying to score illegal drugs to manage his painkiller addiction. No matter how many times she told herself Heath was responsible for his own actions, she couldn't shake the thought that something needed to be done about the smuggling network. Heath aside, there were plenty of reasons to want it gone. Shifter rumors were more frequent, including rumors specifically about shifters smuggling. Then there was the tarnish it was leaving on the shifter community. Shifters had their own code of honor and the smugglers had flouted it blatantly.

Sophia was relieved when a couple walked up to the counter. It derailed the conversation. She busied herself waiting on them. Heath and Daniel made their way to a table nearby, appearing deep in conversation. Vivi waited by the counter. When the couple moseyed away, Vivi rested her hip on the counter and eyed Sophia. "Heath's being mighty quiet about Daniel."

"Yeah, I know. Either I'll hear about it later, or he's fine with Daniel."

Vivi looked over at Daniel and Heath. "I'm pretty sure he can pick up on the obvious. He seems to like Daniel well enough."

Sophia followed Vivi's gaze. Heath was leaning back in his chair, looking comfortable and at ease. Daniel looked much the same. Whatever Heath might think of her and Daniel, he appeared to get along with Daniel, which was a relief. She might be struggling to stare down her own uncertainties, but she wanted Daniel to be accepted by her family.

Vivi turned back to Sophia, the loose braid in her hair swinging over her shoulder. "Heath looks good. He seems almost back to himself, the way he was before the accident."

"I know. I'm so relieved. I just hope he stays this way. My mom isn't going to relax for a good long while."

"I know she's been worried, but I think Heath'll be okay. He looks better than ever."

Another customer approached the counter with yet another right behind. Vivi caught Sophia's eyes. "Catch you later, okay?"

Sophia nodded and stayed focused on taking orders. Vivi made her way to the table where Daniel and Heath were sitting. The after work rush began. By the time things slowed down, Sophia glanced over to see Heath and Vivi had left. Daniel had pulled his laptop out and was busy working. A part of her was thrilled to have him here waiting for her to finish work.

13

Daniel stood in the middle of the living room in his apartment. He'd spent so little time here, it didn't even look lived in. He could easily pack up and move in an afternoon. His mind rolled backwards to the months he was planning his move to Painter. What he'd said to Sophia about his family was true. He'd had a good childhood. The only mar of significance was the heavy burden of his brother's death. He'd been so young, his memories of David were vague. However, his recollection of his parents' pain was vivid. Each had carried the grief of David's death with them to their death. Yet, they'd created a childhood of love and hope for Daniel. He hadn't come to Painter to fill a hole. He'd come to Painter to connect with the shifter side of himself. Discovering his only living uncle might be deep in the smuggling network made him sick, but he was fairly matter of fact about it. While it would have been nice to find family that could mean something to him, he'd found Sophia. She was far, far more meaningful.

He took a breath and strode to the desk. He quickly tucked his back up hard-drive in its small travel case. He'd reached a point with Sophia where he thought he needed to say aloud what was blaring like a trumpet in his heart. He couldn't conceive of ever being without her. After tossing some clothes in a bag, he slung it over his shoulder and left the apartment again. On his way back to Sophia's house, his phone vibrated in his pocket. He tapped the screen on his dash and answered over the speakers.

"Daniel here."

"Daniel, it's Roger Shaw."

"Officer Shaw?"

"You got it. Look, I'm following up after our chat the other day. We've done some more digging on your uncle and were wondering if you'd be open to working with us on this."

He didn't hesitate. "Sure. How about I stop by the station?"

"Sounds great."

"Be there in five."

The line went quiet, and Daniel kept driving toward downtown Painter. He pulled up to the police station and met Roger just inside. A while later, he headed back out. The plan was for him to visit Nelson again and try to rattle him. The police had done their homework and discovered his grandparents' home had been deeded directly to Daniel, not Nelson. Nelson had probably hoped Daniel would never bother to show up in Painter, much less assume the home had bypassed Nelson. Daniel went straight from the police station to the law office of the attorney Lila had told him about.

The law office in question was housed in an old, stately home on a side street in downtown Painter. Daniel walked into the reception area, which held a desk and a few chairs. With no one around, he followed the instructions on the sign and tapped the small bell sitting on the desk. After a few minutes, a door across the hall opened and an older gentleman walked into the room. The man was tall and lanky with silver hair and brown eyes. He held his hand out. Daniel shook it quickly.

"I'm looking for Paul Thornton. I'm Daniel Hayes and..."

"Daniel, Lila Ashworth told me you were in town. I've been planning to call. I'm Paul. Very nice to meet you. Let's meet in my office."

Paul walked past Daniel and opened a door to the side of the desk, gesturing for Daniel to follow him. Paul's office contained a large mahogany desk, a round table with chairs, and bookshelves covering every wall. Two tall windows allowed sunlight to fill the room. They sat at the table. Paul leaned his elbows on the table and eyed Daniel. "You look just like your grandfather when he was younger. Good to see you," Paul said gruffly.

Unsure what to say, Daniel nodded.

"Lila thought you might want to know about your grandparents' will."

"Not because I want to cause any trouble, but it sounds like maybe my uncle isn't abiding by their wishes."

"Most certainly not. Your grandparents left most everything to you. After your older brother died and your parents moved away with you, Nelson went down a bad path. Your grandparents loved him, but they saw how things were going and figured if they wanted to make sure you got what they hoped for, they'd best not put him in charge of it. They didn't leave him without anything. They set up a fund for him that should have carried him through most of his life if he'd been careful. The house, the properties, and the rest were tied up for you. As far as I can tell, Nelson blew through what they left him. He tried to contest the will in court and lost."

Paul leaned back in his chair and sighed. "Even though they left so much for you, I was given strict instructions not to seek you out. Your grandparents loved your mother dearly, and you just as much. They didn't want to cause pain and only wanted you to come here if it was on your terms. I must say, I'm relieved you finally came to Painter. If there's anything I can do, just let me know. I have all the paperwork here so you can access your accounts. As for the house and the property, we have our work cut out for us. I had eviction papers served on Nelson years ago, but he's been playing games. I know he's living there, but he manages to make it look as if it's abandoned. With you here now, I'm thinking we'll be able to get him out of there for good."

Daniel shrugged. "It's not that I don't want him out of there, but I'm not in a rush. We can take it slow. He was pretty cold to me when I stopped by and now I understand why. He lied to me about the house too. Said it was deeded to me after he passed away."

Paul shook his head slowly. "It's sad to see the direction he's taken. It broke your grandparents' hearts." Paul stood up and walked over to his desk. He tugged a stack of files out of his desk and brought them to the table. As he began flipping through them and pulling out documents, Daniel spoke up.

"Right now, I'm hoping to get your back up on the property. I'll try to keep it brief, but the police asked for my help with an investigation involving Nelson."

Paul's sharp brown eyes swung over to Daniel. "Fill me in."

"Long story short, I was with some friends and we stumbled across an old cabin in the woods where they thought some shifter smugglers have been meeting. I'm sure you've heard about the smuggling network..."

"Impossible not to hear about it. It's a damn shame and a tragedy for Painter," Paul added.

"Anyway, I was pretty sure I saw Nelson out there. On

the way back, two shifters came after us. We handled it and brought them into the police station. When I told the police I thought I saw Nelson there, they told me they've suspected he was involved for a while. Officer Shaw called me today and asked if I minded helping them out. They're hoping I can rattle Nelson by pushing the issue on the house. I figured I'd better make sure I had the legal pieces in place."

Paul leaned back in his chair and sighed heavily. "It doesn't surprise me at all to hear Nelson's involved with the smuggling. Since he blew through what money your grandparents left him, I've been curious to know how he's been getting by. Your grandparents would roll over in their graves if they knew about this. They'd be horrified to know he's putting shifters at risk like that." Paul paused and shook his head slowly. "Anyway, you needn't worry about the legal issues. The deed on the property is rock solid. Nelson already knows that, which is why he works so hard to make it look like he's not living there. The records are filed at the local courthouse, and I have copies of everything. Rather than you lugging them around, simply refer Nelson to me if he tries to push the issue. He won't. The police are correct. It will rattle him to have you around and actually know what's going on." Paul smiled, his eyes crinkling at the corners. "I'm not a young man, you know. I wasn't so sure I'd be around if you ever showed up. I can't tell you how good it is to see you and to know you turned out to be the man your grandparents hoped. Your mother was an absolute dear, and your father was a good man. I understood why they left Painter, but they were missed dearly."

Daniel chest tightened, a wave of emotion washing through him. He'd come to terms with the loss of his parents, but he still missed them. It was nice to know they'd been missed by the friends and family they left behind in Painter. He cleared his throat. "I know the feelings were mutual. My mother never stopped talking about how much she missed Painter, which is one of the reasons I finally came here."

"It's good to have you here," Paul said firmly. He paused, his eyes considering. "You might want to know Lila Ashworth has her heart about set on you sweeping her daughter off her feet. Lila's a force to be reckoned with."

Daniel shrugged. If he had his way, Lila would get her wish. "Good to know Lila and I agree. I can't say for certain if I've succeeded at sweeping Sophia off her feet, but I sure as hell aim to try."

Paul chuckled. "Well then, I suppose you don't need to worry about Lila pressuring you then, seeing as you two seem to be in agreement."

DANIEL WALKED up the steps of his grandparents' old home and knocked on the door. With the understanding of why the home appeared vacant outside and in, he felt a twinge of annoyance with Nelson. He supposed he should feel anger, but it was such a childish thing to do. Instead of being smart enough to live reasonably on the money left to him by his parents, Nelson had blown through it in short order and now had to slink about in their old home to avoid being formally evicted.

While he waited for Nelson to answer the door, he glanced around at the overgrown yard. Everything was unkempt. He recalled his mother talking about how much his grandmother loved gardening. While Daniel could dredge up some empathy for Nelson after David's death blew a hole through their family, he couldn't appreciate Nelson's choice to try to weasel his way into living illegally on the old property and purposefully letting it go in an effort to make it look as if he didn't live there.

Just when Daniel lifted his hand to knock on the door again, the door swung open. Nelson stood there, his expression guarded. Daniel had enough sense to know Nelson may have discovered he'd been behind the two shifters who'd been arrested. He and Roger had reviewed his approach. Daniel needed to push Nelson to get the hell off his grandparents' property. The police believed the old cabin Nelson and the other shifters had been seen was on another piece of property that had been deeded to Daniel. Between talking with the police and Paul, Daniel had learned his grandparents' logging business had owned massive tracts of land in and around Painter, in addition to areas all over the West. They'd sold off significant portions of their land holdings before they passed away, but several large holdings had been put in the trust for Daniel. The police were hoping if Daniel forced the issue regarding his grandparents' home, it would push Nelson out to some of the other areas they guessed he was using as meeting points for smuggling operations. Without the main home in Painter to use, Nelson would have more difficulty keeping his whereabouts hidden.

Daniel didn't have to work to dredge up frustration toward Nelson. He eyed Nelson for a long moment and leaned his shoulder against the doorframe. "Thought you might want to know I've met with Paul Thornton."

Nelson's faded blue eyes narrowed and his mouth tightened. "I see. Couldn't trust me to ask, so you went straight to him."

"You lied about the property," Daniel said, getting right to the point.

Nelson shrugged. "Look, the only time your parents bothered to show up in Painter was to pay their respects at my parents' funerals. I was left here to do everything for my parents after your family bolted." The resentment in his tone was mind-boggling. It was as if he couldn't even recognize it was Daniel's parents whose life had been blown apart by the tragic loss of their young son. Daniel didn't doubt it was hard on Nelson and on his grandparents, but none of that softened the crushing blow to his family.

Daniel kept his anger leashed. He needed to stay calm. "No matter how you look at it, it doesn't make it okay you've been lying and taking something that isn't yours. According to Paul, you were left with plenty of money, which apparently you might as well have set on fire for all the good it did you. I came by to let you know I'm aware this property is mine, along with every other piece of property that wasn't sold off. I expect you to be out of here by the end of the week."

Nelson straightened, his expression almost insolent. "You think you can just stroll into Painter after being gone all these years and tell me to get the hell off of my parents' property?" His voice rose with each word, his eyes darkening with anger.

Nelson's anger only strengthened Daniel's resolve. That Nelson believed he was entitled to be angry in this scenario simply illuminated his selfishness and greed. "If that's how you see it, fine. The way I see it, you screwed up your own chances and you've been hoping I'd never show up. I'm here now, and I expect you gone by the end of the week."

At that, Daniel pushed away from the door and started to walk down the porch steps. Nelson's next words sent a hot arc of anger flashing through him. "I'll be gone, but don't think this is the last you'll see of me. You might want to keep an eye on your new girlfriend."

Daniel paused mid-step and turned on his heels to look back at Nelson. "Don't bring her into this. If you do, you'll regret it," he said. It took most of his discipline to keep from shifting and tearing Nelson to pieces. His cat simmered under his skin, but he forced himself to hold back.

Nelson sneered at him. "I might be getting up there in

years, but I'm no kitten. Watch your back." He slammed the door shut.

Daniel remained still for a moment, anger coursing through him in waves. He listened to Nelson's footsteps retreating away from the door, echoing on the hardwood floors in the mostly empty farmhouse. He took a deep breath and slowly descended the stairs. He immediately drove toward downtown, heading to Mile High Grounds to talk to Sophia.

14

"**O**uch!" Sophia yanked her hand away from the side of the espresso machine. They were deep into the morning rush, and she'd carelessly reached to grab a stack of cups and put her hand right under the steamer.

Tommy whipped his head to the side to glance at her. "You okay?"

She cradled her wrist and looked down. An angry slash of red skin glared back at her, instantly throbbing from the burn. "I'm okay. Give me a few though. I need to run this under some cold water."

"You need anything? I can have Josie handle everything for a few minutes," Tommy said, his eyes concerned. His hands kept moving, pulling coffee shots on autopilot.

Sophia shook her head. The strip of skin that had landed under the steam was stinging and burning, but she'd be okay. "Nah. I'm fine. Just give me a few minutes."

She pushed through the half door that led to a small back room. The room contained shelving piled high with bags of coffee beans, baking supplies, and everything else she needed to run Mile High Grounds. A doublewide stainless steel sink sat against a side wall. She stepped to the sink and ran the cool water over her wrist. The water soothed the burn. She sighed as the pain began to ease. With her free hand, she reached into the freezer beside the sink and grabbed some ice. Turning the water off, she wrapped the ice in a clean towel and held it over the burn.

Leaning her hips against the sink, she listened to the hum of customers out front. She heard the bell chime at the door and footsteps making their way to the counter and then behind it. Just when she was wondering who it was, she heard the distinct sound of Daniel's voice.

"Is Sophia here?"

"She's right through there. Make sure she's taking care of the burn she just got," Tommy replied.

The half door swung open, and Daniel stepped through. His eyes swept over her, landing on the towel she held over her wrist. In three quick strides, he was at her side, his hand cupping her elbow as he lifted the towel to check her wrist underneath. "Tommy said you got a burn. How's it feel?"

She shrugged, a curl of warmth snaking through her at the concern in his voice. She was accustomed to taking care of herself. It was strangely comforting to have him so worried over such a small thing. She looked up into his navy eyes, and her pulse kicked up a notch. "It's okay. A little hot, but it's cooling. I wasn't paying attention and stuck my hand right under the steamer."

Daniel carefully placed the towel over the burn again. "Keep that there for a few more minutes. Do you have any bandages here?"

"I don't need..."

He arched a brow. "It's already swelling and probably going to blister. Better keep it covered just to be safe."

She sighed. "Okay, okay. Fine." She gestured to the far corner where a cabinet held the first aid supplies.

Daniel immediately went to the cabinet and pulled out the first aid kit. He returned to her side with ointment, a bandage and gauze. In short order, he gently spread burn ointment on her skin, carefully placed the bandage and loosely taped gauze over it. When he was finished, he leaned against the wall and slid his hands into his jean pockets. He wore his black leather jacket over a black t-shirt. All he had to do was exist, and he was so damn sexy he took her breath away.

"I'm guessing you're still planning to work the rest of the day," he said with a wry smile.

"Daniel, it's minor. I'll take the register and let Tommy and Josie take care of everything else."

His eyes coasted over her. His expression was solemn. Worry coiled inside of her. "What's going on?" she asked.

His shoulders rose and fell with a deep breath. "You know how I mentioned the police asked for my help with Nelson?"

"Yeah. We just talked about it last night. What happened?"

"For the most part, everything went as I would have expected. Nelson got cranky about me calling his bluff on the property. I just came from there. He, uh, he told me to keep an eye on you."

Sophia stepped to stand in front of Daniel. "Don't let him get to you. He can't hurt me. Okay?"

Daniel slid his hands down her shoulders and tugged her into his embrace. He found it nearly impossible to be rational when it came to Sophia's safety. "I know you can take care of yourself, but Nelson plays dirty. I don't trust him, and I just want you to be careful."

His voice was muffled against her hair. She leaned her head back and looked up. "I'll be careful, okay? Don't let this tie you up. Nelson's on the radar of the police and every shifter who gives a damn about getting rid of the smuggling network. He won't be able to do anything or go anywhere without watching his back."

He stroked a hand through her hair and nodded. "I know, but it doesn't make it any easier to hear him threaten you." He dipped his head and caught her lips in a searing kiss. In seconds, she was on fire inside and twining herself against him. The bell chimed in the front, its distinct sound nudging her brain and reminded her where they were. He tore his lips free, his forehead falling against hers. Their breath gusted in unison.

His voice was low and gravelly when he spoke. "I need to tell you something."

She angled her head up, her eyes caught in his navy gaze. "The first time I met you, I knew what my mother meant when she told me I'd know. See, she had to explain a lot to me in a short time about what it meant to be a shifter. She told me shifters had only one true mate, but not every shifter was lucky enough to find theirs. She said if I did, I would know right away. I knew the second I saw you, although it took me a little bit to accept it. What I'm saying is...I love you. I don't want to go another day without making sure you understand how important you are to me."

His words sent her heart flying. Hope spread its wings and soared along with it. Instantly, her cautious side tried to interrupt. It had been a long and rough year. When Daniel walked into her life, all she'd been hoping for was life to be mundane again and everyone in her family to be okay. *Are you really going to have an internal debate? You're being ridiculous. The man who means more to you than any man ever has just told you he loves you and you're wondering if now is the right time. Don't be stupid.*

Sophia shook her head and then laughed softly. There

she went shaking her head again. Daniel's mouth curled at one corner, but he stayed quiet, his eyes intent on her. Every word of his rang in tune with her and what she felt for him. She tried to speak, but emotion clogged her throat. She took a gulp of air and ran her hand down his chest, coming to a stop over his heart. It pounded, strong and steady, under her palm. She finally found her voice. "You are the same to me. I love you."

He dipped his head again. This time his kiss started tender, but as was the case with them, in seconds it was as if flames were licking around them. He slowly softened their kiss, catching her lower lip between his teeth and gently tugging as he pulled away. Josie called out for Tommy to make two lattes, and Daniel chuckled softly. "I suppose I should let you get back to work."

She grinned and shrugged. "I suppose so. Where were you headed next?"

"I told Roger I'd stop by with an update. Then, I was planning to ask if you minded if I worked from your place again today. I've got a few projects to work on, and Daisy could always use the company." His mouth curled up in that half-smile she'd come to love.

"As if you need to ask," she said, her own smile mirroring his.

The half-door swung open, and Tommy stepped through. "Sorry, but I had to get some more coffee beans." He grabbed two bags and immediately returned to the front.

Sophia stepped back. "I suppose we can't huddle back here all afternoon."

Daniel chuckled. "Probably not."

She took a breath. She didn't know why, but she kept hesitating when it seemed pointless to hesitate. After a long moment, she shook her head. Her cheeks heated when she saw Daniel start to smile. She shrugged. "Laugh if you want. It's you. You make me shake my head."

She took another breath. "Anyway, I was thinking was maybe I should let you know it would be okay with me if we just admitted you might be moving in with me."

"We could say that. The lease for my apartment is a summer lease, just until the end of August," he said with that half-smile never wavering.

She nodded, warmth unfurling from her center and spiraling outward. "Well, until then, you don't need to ask me every day about working at my place."

Another low chuckle and he nodded. She started to turn away and walk out front when his hand cupped her elbow. She turned back. His expression had sobered. "Promise me you'll be careful. Would you mind if I plan to meet you for the walk home? I can bring Daisy with me."

Her reflex was to tell him he needn't worry, but she sensed he needed her to give him this. She also knew Nelson didn't have much to lose anymore and that made him far more dangerous. She could hold her own as a shifter, but other shifters had as much power and more than she did. She wasn't stupid enough to think she could fend off Nelson on her own should he choose to attack. So, she met Daniel's concerned gaze and nodded. "Of course. I'll be here until we close down. Tommy will be with me."

"I'll get here a little early. I'll need my evening coffee anyway."

At that, he followed her out front and snagged a coffee from Tommy before he left.

THE FOLLOWING MORNING, Sophia was at the counter with customers lined up to the door. Tommy and Josie were working at high speed to churn out coffees as fast as they could. After a cluster of college students moved aside to wait for their drinks to be ready, she glanced up to find Nelson Weaver at the counter. She knew him on sight, although she couldn't recall the last time she'd seen him. Tension coiled inside as she recalled Daniel's warning about Nelson's vague threat toward her. She wasn't concerned he would do anything here in the middle of her crowded coffee shop and downtown Painter, but she was concerned what his purpose was. If he'd ever set foot in Mile High Grounds before, she'd have been surprised. She kept her expression neutral as she met his eyes. His expression was cold and flat.

She treated him as she treated every customer. "What can I get for you?" she asked with a polite smile.

His eyes roved around the room before coming back to land on her. "I'm not here for coffee. Just came to tell you that you should tell your new boyfriend to back off. Also, tell him to meet me out at the old cabin two o'clock tomorrow afternoon. You know where I mean," he said pointedly. His expression was unchanged, but the threatening undertone was clear in every word.

Bitter anxiety and anger tightened around her chest. She wanted to lash out, but now was not the time and place. She couldn't lose control here and couldn't let Nelson know he'd rattled her. She pushed against the fear, but she couldn't ignore her worry for Daniel and what it meant that he'd played a part in cornering Nelson. She bought herself a moment by greeting a customer walking by before she turned her gaze back to Nelson and nodded. "I'll let Daniel know," she said with forced politeness before turning to the next customer who came to the counter beside Nelson.

Nelson held her gaze for a long moment before turning away and walking back outside.

15

—————

"What?" Daniel asked, his eyes narrowing as he turned to look at her.

"Just what I said. Nelson stopped by Mile High today and asked me to tell you to back off and to meet him tomorrow at the old cabin," Sophia said, repeating what she'd just said. They were sitting on the couch in her living room. They'd finished dinner, and Daisy was napping in the far corner on her giant dog bed.

Daniel simply stared at her for a long moment. "Did he say anything else?" His voice was low and controlled.

"Not really. He was only there for a minute. He told me what I just told you and said I'd know where he meant. In case it's not obvious, I'm pretty sure he knows Vivi and I have been out there."

Daniel was quiet for another few beats. "He made his point by going to you to pass on his message. Fucking asshole. He wants to make sure I know he's willing to go after you." Daniel's eyes had gone dark and stormy.

His arm was thrown across her shoulders, and she was

leaning into the crook of his shoulder. She placed her hand over his and squeezed. "I know you're worried he might do something, but he didn't when he had his chance. I think he's just rattling cages. I'm not sure what I think of you going out to meet him though."

She angled her head back, so she could look over at him. His eyes canted down to hers. "I don't like that he showed up there. If he wanted to talk to me, he knows how to find me. He went to you to make a point. Just promise me you'll be careful."

"Of course! So what are you going to do? Are you going out to the cabin tomorrow?"

Daniel adjusted his arm and stroked his hand through her hair, idly sifting through it. "Don't know yet. I'll talk to Roger before I do anything. If I go, it won't be alone."

Worry slithered through her. Until this situation with Nelson was settled, she would worry. She'd become so accustomed to worrying over the last year that the feeling was familiar. She glanced up at Daniel's profile. He was staring blindly toward the television, not paying the least bit of attention to the news on the screen. Her eyes coasted over the angles of his face—the sharp slashes of his dark brows, the clean line of his nose, the angled cheekbones that sloped down to his sensual mouth. He must have sensed her gaze on him because he swung toward her, capturing her eyes in his. The air around them grew heavy, thick with desire. Lust unfurled like smoke, rising from the embers inside. His hand stroked through her hair and curled around the nape of her neck. His thumb caressed in a slow stroke—back and forth over the beat of her pulse in her neck.

Awareness skated through her when his eyes roamed across her face. It was as if he was tracing her with his touch, yet he didn't lift a finger. With his eyes on her, she pushed up from where she was resting against him and turned to straddle him. She sank her hips down, her breath coming out in a gasp at the feel of his hard shaft against her. She was already wet for him. All it took was the mere thought of touching him, and she melted. She slid her hands down his shoulders, over the corded muscles of his arms. His eyes were dark with desire as he lifted his hand and traced her lips with his thumb.

He slid his other hand under the hem of her t-shirt and up her back. The rough surface of his palm sent sparks skittering up her spine. With subtle pressure, he brought her forward as he met her halfway and caught her lips in a scorching kiss. Heat blazed through her. His kiss was commanding and sent her spinning into the tides of lust rushing through her. Their tongues tangled sinuously. What started as a slow dance shifted gears and became wild and furious. He shoved her shirt up and over, tossing it to the floor. His followed, and she sighed in relief at the feel of his chest against her skin. His palms came around to cup her breasts. He dragged his thumbs back and forth across the black silk, driving her nearly mad with need. Her nipples were tight and achy. Only when a low moan broke from her did he flick his thumb under the clasp and fling her bra to join their scattered shirts on the floor.

His lips traveled down the curve of her neck, blazing a trail of fire. She shifted restlessly against him, frustrated at the layers of clothing between them. His lips closed over a nipple, and she cried out, arching into the wet heat of his mouth. He swirled his tongue around the tight bead of her nipple before biting down sharply, simultaneously relieving the ache of need and notching it higher. While he turned the same maddening attention to her other nipple, she twisted against him and busied her hands, swiftly unbuttoning his jeans and curling her palm over the pulsing heat of his cock.

Suddenly, he lifted his head and gripped his hands on

her hips. In one quick move, he stood with her held firmly in his strong embrace. She squeaked, and his mouth hooked at one corner. He adjusted her in his arms, and she curled her legs around his hips. He carried her to the bedroom and shouldered through the door. Without ever letting her go, he somehow managed to flick the lamp on and stretch her out underneath him. In short order, he dragged her jeans off and kicked his aside. She rested on her elbows and looked up at him. In the shadowed light, the hard planes of his body stood out, every inch of him pure muscle. He left his briefs on and stretched out beside her, his hand tracing a meandering path over her breasts and belly. Her panties were already drenched from her need, and the wet heat kept building and building as he stroked down over the cotton and dragged his fingers back and forth. With each stroke, need coiled tighter and tighter inside.

"Daniel...I need..."

"This?"

His query came just as he hooked a finger and dragged her panties down. Before she could form a reply, he stroked his fingers through her folds and dipped into her channel in a swift plunge. With a muffled cry, she arched into his touch. She managed to drag her eyes open and slip her hand down the front of his briefs, stroking over the pulsing velvet skin of his shaft.

"This," she replied.

With need clawing inside of her, each stroke of his fingers sent shudders through her. It wasn't enough. She wanted all of him. She rolled swiftly to her side and strad-dled him, shoving his briefs down over his hips. His cock rested against her, and she rolled her hips, driving herself wild just to feel him against her. His eyes locked on hers and she slowly rose up. She held still, feeling the head of his cock at her entrance, before she drove her hips down, taking him all the way inside at once.

He gripped her hips as she rode him, savoring every inch of him as he filled her with each roll of her hips. Pressure gathered within, and she toed the edge of ecstasy, chasing it each time he filled her. His grip on her hips tightened when she arched into his strokes. With a quick stroke of his thumb across her clit, she tumbled over the crest, a sharp spike of pleasure followed by shudders that rocked her to her core. His body went rigid underneath her and her name came out in a hoarse cry.

Sophia fell against Daniel. His hands eased their grip and slipped around her. A palm stroked in slow circles on her back. After several moments, she lifted her head and found his eyes waiting for her. He lifted a hand and brushed her tangled hair away from her face. His eyes held a fierce tenderness. He cleared his throat. "This thing with Nelson scares me. I don't like it. I want to lock you up and keep you safe until he's behind bars."

She traced a finger along his eyebrow, smoothing it. Worry fluttered inside of her. While he was busy wanting to keep her safe, she was far more concerned about him. Any threat Nelson made toward her was truly directed toward Daniel, and that scared her. She shoved those thoughts away and focused on what he said. "I know that would make you feel better, but it's not practical. I'm hardly ever alone as it is. The one place I was alone before was when I was home and even then Daisy was always with me. Now that you're here all the time..." Her words trailed off with a smile.

He smiled softly, but it was fleeting. He caught her lips in a quick kiss. "It's just hard. That's all. You might have to be patient with me. If I seem overprotective, well, I suppose I am when it comes to you. No one's ever mattered to me as much as you do."

She traced his other brow. "Nor you to me."

As she dipped her head down to rest against his shoulder, she considered how she could make sure she went to the cabin with Daniel. It didn't have to be only her, but she knew she could handle herself. She knew she should talk to him about it, but she sensed if she mentioned it now, it would only upset him. Instead, she traced circles on his chest with her fingertip as his breathing evened into sleep.

DANIEL STARED at Sophia for a long moment before he swung away. "No."

"You can't tell me not to go! I've been shifting and fighting for my entire life. I know the mountains around here a hell of a lot better than you do. You know it makes sense."

Her words drove through him. He swung back to face her. "I don't care if it makes sense to you. It doesn't make sense to me. I'll talk to Roger, and I won't go alone, but you're not going." His frustration notched higher at the stubborn set of her features.

She crossed her arms and paced back and forth in front of the window. "You can't tell me what to do!"

He stepped in front of her when she paused in her pacing and cupped her shoulders. "Look, I'm not asking you to stay because I think I can control what you do. I just need to know you're going to be safe. If I know you're out there, I just...hell, I just can't deal with that."

He tugged her roughly into his arms and buried his face in her hair. She was stiff at first, but her body softened against him. He felt the rise and fall of her breath before she tipped her head back and stroked her palm over his cheek. Her hand trailed down to rest over his heart. She nodded slowly. "Okay. But promise me you'll ask Heath to go with you. I don't care who else Roger sends, I want Heath with you."

"If I call Heath, you'll stay back?"

She chewed her lip and took another breath before she nodded.

16

Daniel walked beside Heath through the trees. After Daniel conferred with Roger, they'd decided it would be best to have Daniel head out to meet Nelson at the old cabin with the police coming in from another direction. Roger assured him they would only use officers who were shifters and thought Heath was ideal to join Daniel. He'd suggested Nelson would probably consider Heath a weak link due to everything that had happened, which might work in their favor.

At the moment, they were hiking into the mountains before shifting when they were deep enough into the forest. On the drive out, Heath had shared his concern that Sophia and Vivi might be inclined to do their own reconnaissance. Daniel would have liked to think Heath was wrong, but he knew how concerned Sophia was. After she'd agreed not to go, they hadn't discussed it again. He couldn't help the curl of apprehension. He didn't think she'd purposefully mislead him, but he definitely thought she could easily reconsider. As they approached a wide stream, Heath glanced over at him.

"Soph wouldn't come out alone, you know. If she decides to follow us, Vivi will be with her. I'm guessing you asked her not to, but she's got a stubborn streak and she's a hell of a fighter. Soph and Vivi can hold their own. I thought I should mention it, so you don't get surprised if something goes awry and they get flushed out," Heath said.

"How good are the chances they'd show up without letting us know?" Daniel asked, trying to ignore the tension knotting in his chest.

"Better chances than if they let us know," Heath offered with a wry grin. His expression quickly sobered. "Seriously, they can handle themselves fine. Soph and Vivi know these mountains blind. They can fight with the best of them, and they're both fast as hell. I just thought you could use the heads up."

Daniel nodded and took a gulp of the cool forest air. Under the trees, a mix of evergreens and aspen, the forest was shadowed with patches of sun breaking through here and there. They paused beside the stream with its icy, clear water tumbling over rocks, the rushing sound soothing and invigorating at once. Daniel glanced to Heath. "Shall we?"

At Heath's firm nod, they shifted. Daniel had come to savor the rush of power when he shifted. Fur rippled over him in a wave. A sense of strength and power far beyond any human power coursed through him. He stood tall beside the stream and looked around. His eyes and ears were sharper and far more attuned in lion form. He glanced to Heath who stood tall and strong beside him. Heath swung his head side to side before bunching onto his haunches and effortlessly leaping over the stream. Daniel followed, easing to Heath's side as they threaded their way deeper into the mountains.

The cool air ruffled through his fur as they ran. The scents of the forest were sharp. He scented a pair of squirrels just before they began chattering. In what felt like almost no time, they approached the bluff overlooking the valley where the old cabin sat. The plan was for Daniel to approach in plain sight once they scouted the area. Heath would hang back in the tree line, revealing himself only if necessary. As agreed, they paused at the bluff and watched for several long moments. The scent of humans and lions was discernible, but there was no motion around the cabin. They backed away from the bluff and circled around the valley, staying hidden among the trees. As they moved through the trees, they saw three shifters approaching from the opposite side. Heath had assured Daniel he'd be able to confirm who any shifters were. As the shifters saw them and hung back, Heath flicked his tail and nodded, indicating they were the police in shifter form. After a full loop revealed nothing out of the ordinary, Daniel and Heath paused in an area where there was a clear view of the cabin.

Daniel glanced to Heath who nodded slowly, lifting his chin toward the cabin before he leapt silently onto a tree branch and settled in to look across the valley. Daniel moved quietly through the trees and out into the small clearing surrounding the cabin. There was still no motion of any kind. Daniel knew the police were positioned in the trees nearby, at two different corners in view. He slowly approached the cabin. The door hung open, its hinges squeaking in the soft breeze blowing through the valley.

Daniel padded into the cabin and glanced around. It contained a few chairs and a wall of stainless steel storage cabinets. The cabinets were fitted with high-end digital locks. The cabin was a classic frontier cabin. It contained one large front room with a massive cast iron cooking stove in the center of the room. Two small rooms, likely bedrooms, were off to the side. Both rooms were empty save more stainless steel cabinets against the walls. As he circled around, his eyes noted small details—the clear evidence of frequent traffic in the footsteps on the dusty floor. The traffic was a mix of paw prints and a variety of shoe prints. At the moment, no one was here. The tension coiled inside of him tightened. He didn't trust Nelson, so he pondered what Nelson's plan could be.

There was suddenly a rush of sounds in the distance outside. He raced out of the cabin and paused to look around. He could hear the scuffle, but he couldn't see it. As his senses pinpointed the location, he loped across the valley. He could sense Heath moving in the same direction, but Heath remained hidden in the trees. As Daniel got closer to the area, he saw Sophia dash out of the trees, glorious in cat form. She spun around to face the mountain lion behind her, a heavy, muscled cat. Sophia dodged and spun again when the other cat snarled and lunged toward her. A wash of anger and protectiveness coursed through Daniel. He shifted from a jog to a dash. Sophia didn't spare him a glance as she darted toward the other lion and easily swiped her claws across the lion's neck. The other lion roared and batted in her direction, but missed. As Daniel watched, he guessed the lion was Nelson. He almost lumbered in his motion, and it was clear he was aging. He was still quite powerful, but he couldn't match Sophia's speed. Vivi dashed into sight, drawing another shifter out into the open.

If Nelson had intended to stay hidden, he'd underestimated who might come with Daniel. In seconds, between Sophia, Vivi and Heath, it was a fast and furious brawl among the lions. Daniel dashed among them and went straight for Nelson who repeatedly kept trying to corner Sophia. With snarls, hisses and motion around them, Daniel circled Nelson who kept dodging and attacking Sophia. Daniel was unfamiliar with the other two shifters who'd appeared with Nelson. The fight began to drag on. His eyes snagged on a dark stain of blood in Sophia's fur along her shoulder. Anger surged as he leapt toward

Nelson, catching him by the neck and throwing him to the ground. Nelson tore free and bolted through the cluster.

Daniel took chase, his legs bunching under him with every leap. He felt Sophia catch up to him. Nelson had almost crossed the valley. Sophia nudged his shoulder, breaking his stride. Daniel snarled at her, and she snarled right back. He didn't know why, but she was trying to stop him. Ignoring her, he kept running, his eyes on Nelson's tail as it flicked in the air behind him. They crossed into the trees. In seconds, the ground became rocky, small rocks rolling under his paws as he leapt to catch up to Nelson. The sound of rushing water reached his ears, becoming louder with each bounding leap forward. Suddenly, Nelson disappeared out of sight. Daniel was mere seconds behind him and saw the waterfall going over the cliff at the last second. Sophia dashed in front of Daniel, knocking him swiftly to the ground in the edge of the stream. When he leapt back up, he saw her scrambling to catch her footing in the water and watched in horror as she slipped and fell. She was precariously close to the edge of the waterfall and clawed at the wet rocks to keep from falling.

Daniel roared from the fear pounding through him. Sophia was a blur of motion with the water rushing over and around her. Fear and adrenaline driving him, Daniel leapt in front of her and grabbed with his teeth at Sophia as she fell. He barely caught her by the side of the neck. The sound of water rushing through his ears, he started to move only to feel Sophia get caught in the current again. His hold on her loosened as he struggled to remain upright and fought against the force of the water. She clawed wildly and snagged one paw around a boulder. Between her straining to hold herself in place, he gained enough time to get a firmer grip on her. He forced himself to move slowly as he backed away with Sophia gripped firmly in his teeth. Only when they were far enough away from the waterfall did he ease his hold. She shook her head and stood, bedraggled, blood streaked and drenched wet. He roared—his roar an echo of his feelings. Sophia meant too much to him, and pure fury raced through him as he realized how close she'd come to tumbling over the waterfall. His breath bellowed in the forest as his heartbeat finally began to slow and it sank in that Sophia was safe. She stepped past the stream and was waiting for him in the trees.

He glanced back to where the stream sluiced off the cliff, rolling hundreds of feet into a clear pool below. Nelson's form had disappeared into the water. The water eddied in the pool and then rolled over another cliff. All Daniel could see was Nelson's lion lift its head out of the water before he slipped over the next waterfall. Daniel held still beside Sophia. Their breath heaved in the cool air.

17

———————

The following afternoon, Daniel leaned against the wall in Roger Shaw's office. Though Nelson had bolted, his whereabouts currently unknown and his survival in question, the police had come away from yesterday with two more shifters in custody and walked away from the cabin with a haul of their drug supply. The two shifters had been happy to jabber away once it became clear their main source of income had disappeared over a cliff.

It was still smarting Daniel that Nelson had escaped. Sophia had explained that unless he managed to get out of the water, he had a rough ride downhill with the waterfalls he'd tumbled over being the easier part of his fall. She'd also explained the reason she'd tried to slow Daniel was she feared Nelson hoped to trap him into falling over the cliff. Every time Daniel thought about the fact Sophia almost followed Nelson over the cliff, his heart skipped a few beats. The thought of losing her terrified him. He hadn't yet brought himself to talk about it. When she'd tried to say something last night, all he could do was shake his head.

For now, Roger leaned back in his chair and looked to Daniel. "I know you're not happy Nelson's status is in question, but we drove the biggest wedge yet into the smuggling network. Nelson was the mastermind and used your grandparents' old properties for storage and checkpoints. Since you inherited all of their properties, with your permission, we can search them all. They sold a lot off, but I plan to check the sales and follow up with the new owners. Nelson had a lot of time on his hands, so it's reasonable to guess he had time to scout all of them. We'll get to work, but now we have a way to rattle the network at its core. The shifters relied on these remote storage locations for transfers and drop offs. Without them, we can disrupt the entire network."

"You have my permission to search any of the properties I own. If you need something in writing, just tell me what I need to do." He paused, his gut churning every time he thought about Nelson going after Sophia. As Heath had said, she held her own, but it didn't change the beat of anger that pulsed through him. "And what will you do to find Nelson?"

Roger's eyes narrowed, and he steepled his fingers under his chin. "We'll keep looking. I've already sent some guys out to follow the stream all the way down. If he survived, we won't find him right away. It'll take some time to scout him out. I'd tell you not to look, but I know you will. I'd appreciate it if you'd keep us in the loop, so we know where you're searching and when."

Daniel nodded tightly. "Will do. I'm just flat pissed he managed to bolt."

Roger shook his head. "We all are. You can thank Sophia for slowing you down just enough to keep you from running right over the waterfall with him. She knows those woods by heart, so she knew where he was headed."

Daniel sighed and shrugged. "I know. I should thank her, but she almost fell over after him trying to get me out of the way. I'm not going to feel like this is over until we know if he's dead or alive. If he's alive, we need to find him."

"Our shifters can track him as far as he goes, so we've got a damn good shot at finding him if he survived."

"Right, well, I'm headed over to meet Sophia at work. Let me know what you need to take a look at the properties."

"Will do. I'll check on it and get back to you."

Roger's phone rang as Daniel turned to leave. He gave a quick wave and picked up the phone.

SOPHIA HANDED over a coffee to a customer and turned back to the register to find Heath leaning against the counter. "Hey Soph, can I get a mocha latte?"

"You can always get a mocha latte." She tossed a grin his way before calling the order out to Tommy.

Heath's green eyes coasted over her. "You don't look any worse for the wear."

He was referring to the lion fight the other afternoon. The only damage she'd sustained was a deep scratch along her shoulder. It was sore, but otherwise, she was fine. She shrugged. "It wasn't so bad. Though I can't convince Daniel of that."

"Leave it alone. He gets to worry," Heath said with a small smile.

"He does?"

"Yup. He loves you."

"You sound pretty confident about that."

"I'd be willing to bet he's told you the same. I know

what I see. I had my reservations at first, but he's good for you."

Her cheeks heated and warmth spread through her. Heath tended to hold his thoughts to himself, so if he had something to offer, he meant it. It meant more than she could say to have him support her relationship with Daniel. Tears sprung to her eyes. Heath cocked his head to one side. "Hey Soph, I didn't mean to make you cry."

She shook her head and swiped at her eyes. "They're good tears. We haven't had much time to talk with everything going on. Daniel, well, he's..." She paused and tried to gather her words.

Heath's mouth quirked in a half-smile. "He's the one for you. It's plain as day. Nothing more needs to be said."

"I think he's pissed at me for following you guys out there yesterday."

Heath was quiet for a few beats and then shrugged. "Probably so. I warned him you and Vivi would probably show up. Even if he is pissed, it doesn't change how he feels."

"I know, but I've got to find a way to explain I'm sorry, but I'm not sorry."

Heath arched a brow. "Sorry, not sorry? That's confusing."

"Well, I'm sorry I scared him, but I'm not sorry I went. We needed to be there. If we weren't, they would have outnumbered you guys."

"You don't need to explain it to me. Just try to understand why he might be upset."

At that moment, the bell chimed when the door opened and Vivi strolled through. Her dark hair hung in tousled waves around her shoulders. She pushed her sunglasses up on her forehead, her eyes widening and a grin spreading across her face when she saw Heath. Sophia watched as Heath turned toward Vivi, his easy manner disappearing and tension rolling through him. Sophia pondered what that might mean as Vivi strode to him and flung her arms around him. Vivi was a bold and affectionate friend. With Heath's nature to be reserved, Vivi treated him as most didn't. When Vivi dropped her arms, a subtle flush crested on Heath's cheekbones.

Sophia didn't have time to consider the brief interaction when Daniel pushed through the door with Daisy walking at his side. Daisy had become so attached to Daniel, he didn't even need to bother with a leash. She simply followed him wherever he went. Her stately gaze locked onto Sophia as they approached the counter. Sophia stepped from behind the counter and went to them. Daniel caught her lips in a quick kiss before stroking his hand down her back and turning to greet Heath and Vivi. Sophia petted Daisy's head while she leaned into Daniel's shoulder.

A while later, they walked outside the coffee shop, pausing by the door with Vivi and Heath. The sun was dipping down behind the mountain ridge in the distance, its rays stretching skyward with streaks of gold breaking through swirls of orange and red. Heath threw his arm over her shoulder and squeezed her quickly.

"Thanks for the coffee." He stepped away, his eyes glancing past Vivi before landing on Daniel. "Give me a call when you want to work on that roof. I'd be glad to help."

Daniel nodded as he curled his hand around Sophia's. She savored every little touch and bit back a sigh at the strength and warmth of his grip. She canted her eyes up, arching a brow in question.

"When I went out to the farmhouse to let the police take a look around, I noticed a few leaks in the roof. Nelson's been letting the place fall apart around him, so there's a ton of work to do," Daniel said in response to her unspoken question.

"Are you thinking of actually moving out there? It's a beautiful place." Vivi commented, her eyes catching Sophia's. "You two would have a lot more room than you do now, and Daisy would love being able to roam around out there."

Daniel shrugged. "I'm not sure. Whether I keep the place or sell it, it needs to be repaired."

"Like I said, I'm happy to help with whatever you need," Heath said as he started to turn away. "I'll catch you all tomorrow." With a wave, he tucked his hands in his pockets and began walking down the sidewalk, his silhouette dark against the setting sun.

Vivi dropped a kiss on Sophia's cheek and whirled away. "Hey, wait!" she called out. She jogged to catch up to Heath and slipped her hand through his elbow.

Daisy nudged Sophia's hip. Sophia stroked her head and glanced up to Daniel. She recalled Heath's suggestion that she try to understand why Daniel might have been upset. She needed to clear the air. "For what it's worth, I know we haven't talked about it, but I understand why you might be pissed off I went to the cabin with Vivi after I said I wouldn't."

He was quiet and then nodded slowly. "I get why you went. But dammit! You almost fell over the waterfall along with Nelson. I've been trying not to think about it, but..."

She stepped closer and stroked a hand down his arm. "I couldn't *not* go. I didn't trust Nelson. I'm sorry I didn't just tell you I was going no matter what. I'm not sorry I went though."

His shoulders rose and fell with a deep breath. She could feel the tension in him, but she waited, ignoring the urge to over-explain. He finally nodded slowly. "Can we agree that if anything like this happens again, you'll be straight with me?"

"It wasn't like I purposefully lied when I said I wouldn't

go. I meant it at the time. Then you left to go meet Heath and I freaked out, so I changed my mind. I promise next time, I'll let you know either way. Even if it means you're pissed off."

He glanced down, his eyes somber. "You scared me to death when you almost fell over that damn waterfall."

"But I didn't," she said softly. She stroked her hand up his arm and curled it around his neck, pulling him down to meet her lips.

He paused, his lips a whisper away from hers. "It's only because you mean just about everything to me," he said before he crushed his lips to hers.

Seconds later when she'd all but melted in his arms, he pulled back. With hot, liquid need sliding through her veins and her pulse pounding in tune with his, she glanced up. His eyes were waiting for her, fire and understanding within them.

After several beats of her heart, she found her voice again. "Are we walking home?"

Daniel's blue gaze held hers. She recalled the first day she'd seen him and how his eyes had called to her. His voice was low and gruff when he spoke. "That's what I figured. Daisy expects dinner soon, you know."

She grinned. "Right. Okay, home it is." At that, they began to walk home, Daniel's hand warm around hers.

EPILOGUE

Sophia stood by the kitchen windows at the farmhouse. She held a steaming mug of coffee cupped in her palms and looked out over the field outside. Snow fell softly, the first snow of the season even though it was still early autumn. In the mountains, it could snow even in the summer at high elevations, usually nothing more than a dusting though. At the sound of footsteps, she turned away from the window. Daniel entered the kitchen, and her breath caught in her throat. He wore jeans, which hung low on his hips, and nothing else. His muscled chest and abdomen were mouth-watering as always. His gaze catching hers, he ran a hand through his tousled dark hair. He came to her side and slipped a hand around her waist, pulling her close.

"Morning," he said.

He slowly lifted the coffee cup from her hands and set it on the table beside them before dipping his head and catching her lips in a kiss. In a flash, heat suffused her. His tongue swept inside, tangling with hers briefly before he lifted his head. His eyes were still sleepy. His sensual smile weakened her knees.

"Good morning. It's snowing," she said with a nudge of her head toward the window.

He looked over her shoulder. "So it is." His arms slid free, and he padded across the floor to the coffee pot and poured himself a cup.

After he took several slow swallows, he strode to the table and lounged in a chair. She sat opposite him and glanced out at the falling snow, which coated the field like fairy dust. "So, what's the plan today?"

Daniel gave her a long look, the heat of his gaze warming her. "Well, we've moved everything there is to move. I suppose all we have left to do now is unpack."

In the months since Nelson had disappeared, life had been busy. The police had continued to make inroads into disrupting the smuggling network. Their hunches about the properties had been accurate. They'd systematically searched and taken down multiple locations used for storage and transfer of the drugs, some on properties Daniel had inherited and others on properties that had been sold off, but were so remote it was possible for shifters to stealthily access them with little concern of being detected. The network had largely been isolated in Painter, yet there was the lingering question over Nelson's whereabouts. With shifters having searched for him, all were confident he had survived as no corpse had been found—human or mountain lion. His scent had been lost deep in the mountains over a river crossing.

After Daniel and Heath had done some basic repairs on the farmhouse, Sophia and Daniel made plans to move out here. Though Nelson had spent time here, he'd left little remnants of his presence. The farmhouse was lovely. Sophia had spent many an afternoon clearing the overgrown yard. She'd have to wait until next spring to see the flowers she'd found hiding under weeds and vines.

Daniel slid his hand across the table and curled his palm into hers, his thumb stroking slowly across the back of her hand. "How do you feel now we're here?"

At that moment, Daisy ambled into the kitchen and over to the table. She slipped her chin onto Sophia's thigh, her usual request for a greeting. Sophia stroked her with her free hand and looked back to Daniel. A sense of possibility soared within. "I feel just right."

$\sim$

DANIEL WATCHED Sophia's green eyes brighten as she looked over at him. He'd come to Painter not even looking for love and it had slammed into his life in the form of Sophia. Her black hair fell in loose locks around her shoulders. Her green gaze held his, her eyes sparkling. He couldn't help it, but every time she was near, he was barely holding onto the reins of desire that pounded hard and fast through his body. He took a gulp of coffee and set it back down on the table.

He didn't like the unsettled feeling that rose to the surface occasionally when he wondered where Nelson was and when he would surface. Aside from that, he was more content than he'd ever been. The connection he felt with Sophia was unlike anything he'd experienced or even thought he could experience. To have her here with him in the home his mother once loved brought him full circle inside, linking his past to his present.

Her family had brought him fully into their fold. He hadn't known he was hoping to find a sense of belonging, but he'd found it. The mountain lion within him was fully at home here, as was the human within him. Sophia had turned to look out the window. His eyes traced her profile, lingering on her full lips. Her cheeks flushed as he looked at her, and she turned with a half-smile. "Yes?"

"Just right sounds good to me."

She squeezed his hand and slid hers free, standing to step to the coffee pot and fill her coffee again. When she returned, he caught her around the waist and pulled her into his lap. She giggled and relaxed against him. He tucked a lock of hair behind her ear and reached into his pocket. He held his palm between them, balled into a fist. He cleared his throat and found he couldn't seem to form words. He simply uncurled his hand. In the months after his father passed away, his mother had gone on a spree of giving items away. She'd given him his grandmother's wedding ring at the time, telling him the ring would bless him. The ring was white gold, engraved with a twined pair of wild roses on the inside of the band. He'd learned by chance from Sophia's mother that she loved wild roses and cultivated those she found. When she'd uncovered a cluster on the corner of his grandparents' property, he'd known he needed to make official what he already knew—that he intended to be with her forever and couldn't even contemplate any other reality for his life.

His heart pounded, hard and fast against his ribcage, as he waited to see her response. Her gaze fell to the ring, glinted with the sun rising through the snowy morning. "Oh!" Her eyes flew to his, bright with the sheen of tears. "Is this...?"

He cleared his throat and managed to form words. "It's my grandmother's wedding band. My mother told me I would know who to give it to. I love you, and I can't imagine anything other than a life with you, so I thought maybe I'd ask you to marry me."

"Maybe?"

"Not maybe. One hundred percent certain. I've never

done this, so I haven't had much practice. Let me say it this way. Marry me, please. If you're not..."

She placed her finger over his lips and lifted the ring from his palm, holding it up to the light from the window. Her eyes met his. "Yes, yes, yes," she said softly. She lifted her chin. He met her halfway and crushed his lips to hers. He tried to keep his kiss gentle, but there was no gentle to the passion swirling around them.

Thank you for reading The Lion Within - I hope you loved Sophia & Daniel's story!

For more steamy, small town shifter romance, Heath & Vivi's story is next Lion Lost & Found. A friends to lovers story, Heath & Vivi's romance is epic. Don't miss Heath's story!

Keep reading for a sneak peek!

Be sure to sign up for my newsletter for the latest news, teasers & more! Click here to sign up: http://jhcroixauthor.com/subscribe/

"Hey Vivi!"

Vivian Sheldon turned in the direction of the voice calling her name and spotted a table full of tipsy college students. She quickly grabbed a tray from the counter and set to pouring several house draft beers. She knew if she showed up to the table with only one, she'd be turning right back around for more.

Within moments, she slipped from behind the bar at Quinn's Restaurant and Bar and delivered the beers to the table in question. Her foresight in bringing extra beers was rewarded with a hefty tip.

"Thanks Vivi! You're a mind reader," one of the guys declared as she turned away.

She offered a quick grin and headed back behind the bar. She worked pick-up shifts at Quinn's usually a few nights a week. She'd have preferred not to, but she always needed the money. As a single mother to her seven-year old daughter, Julianna, she tended to barely scrape by month-to-month. If it weren't for her mother babysitting for free whenever she needed it, she didn't know what she'd do.

Quinn's was packed tonight, which was its usual state. Quinn's had been a fixture in Painter, Colorado for many years. It served classic pub fare with some modern updates to the menu in terms of more creative burgers and other items. It catered to pretty much everyone from the college students to locals and tourists who passed through town for skiing in the winter, or hiking in the summer.

Vivi slipped behind the bar again, which ran the full length of the back wall. She quickly wiped down a spill on the polished wooden counter, its surface worn and grooved from years of use. She moved on to serving customers who lined the bar, occasionally glancing around the room to see if any tables needed drinks. Round tables were scattered throughout the center of the large room with booths lining the walls. Pool tables and card tables were through an archway to another room.

The night passed by quickly. By the time Vivi was walking out at midnight, she had earned enough in tips to pay her electric bill. She waved goodbye to the staff who would stay until closing in another two hours, stepped out into the cool autumn air and took a slow breath. The street-lights lining Painter's streets were on, lighting her way home. Painter, Colorado was a small town nestled in the Rocky Mountains. Vivi didn't live far from downtown, so she usually walked to and from town. She stood on the sidewalk for a moment before she began walking, the noise from Quinn's gradually fading as she walked away.

She passed by mostly darkened storefronts with a few restaurants and bars still open. Painter was home to a state university and a ski resort, which kept the small town from becoming too sleepy. She had forgotten to bring a jacket and shivered in the cooling air. Autumn in the Rockies could mean somewhat warm days and rather chilly nights with the temperature varying from day to day until winter took hold. She heard footsteps in the distance approaching her. Her senses sharpened, and she scented the man following her. He wasn't a shifter, which was a relief because it meant if she needed to she could easily fend him off. The downside was she might potentially terrify him.

Vivi had been born a mountain lion shifter into a family of shifters. Shifters blended easily into the world, shifting only when necessary or when desired. Painter happened to be a stronghold for shifters out West, but shifters were everywhere. They had many advantages in the West since wild mountain lions existed in healthy populations here. If a shifter in lion form was sighted in the forest, they were assumed to be a wild mountain lion. Back East, where mountain lion shifters were born out of desperation to save their kind, there was a different set of challenges since mountain lions were believed extinct in the East. As important as secrecy was for shifters, Vivi never took her safety for granted. Revealing herself was something she only did when she chose. She hoped it wouldn't be necessary now as she listened to the footsteps getting closer and closer.

Just when she considered it might be best if she ducked into one of the open bars up ahead, a man walked out of the very door she'd been eyeing. Heath Ashworth's profile was instantly recognizable to her. He stood in the shadowed light and glanced around, his eyes narrowing when he saw her. He immediately turned toward her and began walking in her direction, his stride long and loose. As he approached, he caught her eyes. "Wait here," he said.

She stopped on the sidewalk and turned to look behind her. The man who'd been following her slowed as Heath approached him. Heath leaned over and spoke in the man's ear. Now that she was close enough, she could see the man was young and clearly intoxicated. He weaved back and forth on his feet as he stood in front of Heath. Heath stood tall again. When the man remained still, wobbling slightly, Heath gently placed his hands on the man's shoulders and turned him around. With a little push, the man began walking back down the sidewalk. As he passed by a lighted bar, he stumbled through the door.

Heath turned around and walked back, coming to a stop in front of her. Her pulse started to race, and she tried to tamp it down. Heath was her best friend's older brother, and she'd fought a crush on him since they were teenagers. At thirty-two years old, Heath was three years older than she and her best friend Sophia. Vivi had hidden her crush from Sophia all those years ago and somehow managed to convince herself it was over when Heath enlisted in the Marines and left Painter. She rarely saw him, but for his brief visits home, for many years. About a year and a half ago, he came home for good.

In the years Heath was gone, she'd tried to bury her youthful crush and fancied herself in love with Julianna's father. That had turned out to be nothing more than a case of some serious wishful thinking. After Julianna was born, her father quickly faded out of sight. For the first few years of Julianna's life, he popped up here and there, but Vivi hadn't heard from him in over three years. She'd learned her lesson well and hadn't dated in years.

Right here, right now, in downtown Painter, Heath stood before her and every fevered fantasy she'd had about him when she was a teenager came roaring to the fore. Heath was all kinds of tall, dark and mysterious, even though she'd known him as long as she could remember. He had a body of pure muscle with the simmering power of a mountain lion shifter. His dark hair teased the edges of the denim jacket he wore. His green eyes flicked down to hers.

Okay, Vivi. Now would be the time to get a hold of yourself. You cannot start wishing for the impossible. Heath is not inter-ested in you, so don't give yourself crazy ideas. As soon as she finished that thought, she glanced up into his eyes again and what she saw there made her wonder. If it were anyone other than Heath, she'd have sworn she saw desire darkening his gaze. But this was Heath, and she was nothing more than an overworked single mother who was barely getting by and his sister's best friend who he treated with the same brotherly affection.

"Don't think that guy meant any harm. He's young and drunk and saw a pretty girl walking down the street," Heath said.

His husky voice was like a rough caress. It sent hot shivers through her. She tried to focus on what he said. "Oh, right. Yeah, I wasn't too worried, but I'm glad you happened to be around."

Heath nodded. "Wouldn't have thought you'd be worried," he said with a half-smile. "It's not your style."

She bit her lip and tried, oh she tried, to get her body to behave, but it was as if flames had encircled them. The air was so cool, and she was so hot inside. Heat suffused her and her pulse kept racing unchecked, no matter how hard she tried to slow it. She shivered at the contrast. Heath's eyes narrowed before he shrugged out of his jacket.

"You're cold. Here, this'll help."

He stepped closer to her and swung the jacket over her shoulders, his arms caging her as it settled around her. The denim was warm and held his scent. She had to close her eyes to try to gain control of the desire surging through her. When she opened them again, he was still there, inches away from her. His hands had come to rest on her upper arms. He slid them down, his touch sending an electric current swirling through her. Her pulse rocketed and her breath became shallow when she met his eyes.

His palms reached her chilled hands. His hands, warm and strong, curled around hers, imparting his heat to her. Just when she wondered what she should say to snap this moment, he freed one of her hands and took a step closer.

He was so close now that when she took a breath, her breasts rose and brushed against his chest. She flushed straight through when she realized he could feel her peaked nipples through her t-shirt. Something flickered in the back of his eyes. Before she could ponder it, he slid his hand into her hair and dipped his head.

When his lips were but a breath away from hers, he whispered, "I've been wanting to do this for too damn long."

His lips met hers, and any pretense of thought dissolved into the desire pounding through her. He didn't hesitate. He fit his mouth over hers, and she lost her mind. At her gasp, his tongue swept inside and need thundered through her. She arched into him, so overtaken by sensation she couldn't think and moved entirely on instinct. Her tongue slid against his as she kissed him with everything she had. His arm slipped around her back and pulled her against him. She felt the heat of his erection pressing into her belly. Hot, liquid need pooled between her legs. She slid her hands up his chest, savoring the feel of his hard muscles under her touch.

The sound of a car coming down the street filtered into her consciousness. The bright headlights arced across them. Heath tore his lips free. Awareness slid through her. She scrambled to gather herself. When she looked up, Heath's eyes were right there waiting. *Oh my God, oh my God, oh my God! What the hell were you thinking? You kissed Heath! You have to play it cool somehow. It was just a kiss. Probably means nothing to him. Take a nice deep breath and...*

Heath's hand loosened in her hair, and he slowly freed it before brushing a lock away from her forehead and tucking it behind her ear. Every touch struck sparks under the surface of her skin.

His eyes were somber as he looked down at her. He appeared to be considering his words. Frantic, she filled the silence. "Look, that was just a kiss. We weren't thinking. You don't need to worry I'll..."

He shook his head sharply. "I wanted to kiss you," he said bluntly. "You don't have to brush it off."

She hadn't realized she'd been holding her breath until it came out in a whoosh. Her hands were still on his chest, and she could feel the fast beat of his heart under one of her palms. "Oh, um... Oh."

Wow, brilliant, Vivi. Think you could say 'oh' one more time?

She mentally sighed and glanced up again. His eyes held a glint of amusement, but he was quiet. She took a deep breath, the cool air soothing her nerves just enough so she could think. "Okay, I won't try to brush it off. It's, uh, unexpected, and I'm not sure what you're thinking."

"I'm thinking what I said. I've wanted to kiss you for too damn long, so I finally did."

HEATH LOOKED DOWN AT VIVI, his heart pounding so hard, it reverberated through his body. She took another breath, which he wished she wouldn't. They were on Main Street in downtown Painter in full view of anyone who drove by. He could only take so much of the feel of her tight nipples against his chest. He wasn't sure if he'd lost his mind by kissing her, but he wasn't going to lie. If there was one thing he'd learned in the last year and half, honesty was the only way to go.

Vivi's dark hair fell around her shoulders. It gleamed where the streetlights caught it. Her blue eyes were bright against her fair skin. His eyes roamed over her face—the arch of her dark brows, her high cheekbones slanting down to her bow-shaped mouth, and the subtle vulnerability hiding deep in her eyes. It was that which made his heart clench. He remembered Vivi when she was younger, almost always with Sophia, and so bold, brash and bright. When he returned to Painter after over a decade in the military, it was as if her light had dimmed. He hadn't known how much he relied on her spark until it wasn't so bright.

What he'd said was true. Many years ago, he'd had a few youthful fantasies about her, but he'd swatted them away. It wasn't exactly kosher to lust after his little sister's best friend. A decade in the military has pushed any fantasies beyond brief, purely physical relationships far out of his mind. The last year had nearly broken him. A life-changing car accident sent him to the hospital. He'd left the hospital and cycled through several surgeries to repair his shattered femur. In a fog on painkillers, he'd stumbled around. Occasionally when the fog lifted, he'd see Vivi and wish he could have a chance to explore the fierce pulse of desire he felt for her. Until the last few months when he'd been forced to face his accidental painkiller addiction and how low it brought him, he hadn't felt worthy of anyone. Most certainly not worthy of Vivi—she was strong, loyal, caring, and simply spectacular.

He took a breath and tried to get his body back under his control. He eased his hold on her, though it took an enormous amount of discipline, and took a half step back. He needed the distance, but he couldn't bring himself to stop touching her, so he left his hand resting on her low back. He underestimated just how much he'd want to slide his hand over the curve of her luscious bottom and had to take several slow breaths to maintain control.

Vivi's eyes had fallen, but she lifted them again. Her gaze was clear and direct. "How long is too damn long?" she asked.

He thought for a moment. "Well, there are two answers to that. There's the one where I tell you maybe I thought about kissing you back when you were still in high school." When her eyes widened, he couldn't help the smile that curled the corner of his mouth. "There's the other one where I tell you it was more than that this last year or so. I haven't really been in a place to do anything about it until now."

His chest tightened at what his own words meant. When he heard them aloud, they held a potency he hadn't contemplated. Much as a part of him wanted to run and hide, he held his ground. He was done running from himself, and he sure as hell wasn't going to run from a damn kiss. Even if the kiss was with one of the best women he knew, and even if it scared the hell out of him because it felt so damn good.

Vivi was quiet for several beats, a flush staining her cheeks. One of her hands fell from his chest. She started fiddling with the silver charm bracelet on her wrist. She took a gulp of air before she spoke. "Okay then. That clears it up."

"How about you?"

Another few beats passed, and she took another gulp of air. "Okay, you were honest, so I'll be honest. I suppose I have two answers as well. The first is I might have had more than a few times when I thought about kissing you back in high school. The second is life happened and then you came home again..." she paused, the soft clink of the charms on her bracelet audible while she looked up at him. "...and I've thought about you a lot more."

What he wanted to do was lift her in his arms and find the first place he could to bury himself inside of her, but he wasn't after quick satisfaction. Not with Vivi. He wanted the time to see what lay between them and if it meant as much as he suspected. So, he shackled his impulses and slowly eased his hand off her waist.

"Are you walking home?" he asked.

At her nod, he continued. "I'll walk with you."

They walked through the quiet night. At some point

along the way, he reached for her hand. When they walked up the steps to her house, he looked down and allowed himself one small moment. He dipped his head and caught her lips in a quick kiss. Just that, and it took all of his willpower to pull back.

After she closed the door and locked it behind him, he walked down the stairs and returned to where he'd left his car. His lion simmered, the shackling of his desire went against every grain of the lion side of his shifter self. The chilly, quiet night settled him and by the time he made it to his car, the heat inside had begun to abate.

AVAILABLE NOW!

Lion Lost & Found

Go here to sign up for information on new releases: http://jhcroixauthor.com/subscribe/

FIND MY BOOKS

Thank you for reading The Lion Within! I hope you enjoyed the story. If so, you can help other readers find my books in a variety of ways.

1) Write a review!
2) Sign up for my newsletter, so you can receive information about upcoming new releases & receive a FREE copy of one of my books: http://jhcroixauthor.com/subscribe/
3) Like and follow my Amazon Author page at https://amazon.com/author/jhcroix
4) Follow me on Bookbub at https://www.bookbub.com/authors/j-h-croix
5) Follow me on Instagram at https://www.instagram.com/jhcroix/
6) Like my Facebook page at https://www.facebook.com/jhcroix

Protected Mate
Chosen Mate
Fated Mate
Destined Mate
A Catamount Christmas
The Lion Within
Lion Lost & Found
Swoon Series
This Crazy Love
Wait For Me
Break My Fall
Truly Madly Mine
Into The Fire Series
Burn For Me
Slow Burn
Burn So Bad
Hot Mess
Burn So Good
Sweet Fire
Play With Fire
Melt With You
Burn For You
Crash & Burn
Brit Boys Sports Romance
The Play
Big Win
Out Of Bounds
Play Me
Naughty Wish
Diamond Creek Alaska Novels
When Love Comes
Follow Love
Love Unbroken
Love Untamed
Tumble Into Love

Christmas Nights

Last Frontier Lodge Novels

Christmas on the Last Frontier

Love at Last

Just This Once

Falling Fast

Stay With Me

When We Fall

Hold Me Close

Crazy For You

Just Us

ACKNOWLEDGMENTS

Each and every book is possible due to the incredible support from my family who cheers me on. Special thanks to my husband for helping me keep life in perspective and making sure I remember what's important. My editor, Laura Kingsley, edits with my readers in mind and insists I keep my eye on the story. Claire Tan at CT Cover Creations takes every cover up a notch - many thanks for the beautiful covers she created for this series! Always, a bow of thanks to my readers without whom none of these books would exist. Your support humbles me.

xoxo
    JH Croix

ABOUT THE AUTHOR

USA Today Bestselling Author J. H. Croix lives in a small town in the historical farmlands of Maine with her husband and two spoiled dogs. Croix writes contemporary romance with sassy women and alpha men who aren't afraid to show some emotion. Her love for quirky small-towns and the characters that inhabit them shines through in her writing. Take a walk on the wild side of romance with her bestselling novels!

Places you can find me:
jhcroixauthor.com
jhcroix@jhcroix.com